Soldier Boy

THE WAR BETWEEN MICHAEL & LUCIFER

by

Raymond Dennehy

Trafford
PUBLISHING

Cover photograph: *Archangel Michael*

© iStockphoto/Monika Wisniewska

Cover design by Roxanne Mei Lum

Order this book online at www.trafford.com/07-1433
or email orders@trafford.com

Most Trafford titles are also available at major online book retailers.

Note for Librarians: A cataloguing record for this book is available from Library
and Archives Canada at www.collectionscanada.ca/amicus/index-e.html

ISBN: 978-1-4251-3652-9

*We at Trafford believe that it is the responsibility of us all, as both individuals
and corporations, to make choices that are environmentally and socially sound.
You, in turn, are supporting this responsible conduct each time you purchase a
Trafford book, or make use of our publishing services. To find out how you are
helping, please visit www.trafford.com/responsiblepublishing.html*

*Our mission is to efficiently provide the world's finest, most comprehensive
book publishing service, enabling every author to experience success.
To find out how to publish your book, your way, and have it available
worldwide, visit us online at www.trafford.com/10510*

 www.trafford.com

North America & international
toll-free: 1 888 232 4444 (USA & Canada)
phone: 250 383 6864 • fax: 250 383 6804 • email: info@trafford.com

The United Kingdom & Europe
phone: +44 (0)1865 722 113 • local rate: 0845 230 9601
facsimile: +44 (0)1865 722 868 • email: info.uk@trafford.com

10 9 8 7 6 5 4

For My Beloved Children

Mark, Bridget, Andrea and Rosalind

CONTENTS

FOREWORD

What I have written herein may be described as fiction, fantasy, frolic, all at once. Yet, like a novice tight-rope walker who teeters precariously to and fro, my portrayals of Michael and Lucifer in their verbal jousting probes through their banter to find a reality about angels and about Lucifer's reason for defying his Lord and creator with the words, "I will not serve." If Lucifer was the most intelligent and magnificent of all God's creatures (that's the tradition I've drawn upon), then surely he would have understood in advance that not only was rebellion against his creator doomed to failure from the start but that he himself would be banished into eternal misery to boot. Why, then, did he do it? Tradition tells us that pride led to the most outrageous display ever of rebellion. I offer the reader a more complex account.

Throughout the writing of this book, I have managed to remain true to my initial commitment not to revisit what Thomas Aquinas, Dante, Milton, or C.S. Lewis had to say about angels, their behavior, and Lucifer's rebellion. Why? My Irishman's imagination longed to soar and that meant it had to be unfettered. I did use Milton's account of the battle between Michael and Lucifer because I wanted an account that captured the clash and clang of the fight and nowhere is that depicted better than in Milton's verses. I also consulted Matthew Bunson's marvelous book, *Angels A to Z*, to get some angels' names and to find what tasks the various traditions assigned them. If this book has made any contribution to angelology, it is perhaps my introduction of the angels, Pablo and Ling. After all, why should the Hebrews and Babylonians have the lock on angelic names?

I am grateful to my former students, Sharon Tyree and Katherine Knapp, my colleague and friend Ed Kaitz and his wife, Rachel, and our philosophy department program assistant, Annmarie Belda for comments and encouragement. I am also indebted to Roxanne Mei Lum for designing the cover even though she had better things to do. Finally, I owe thanks to Babette Francis for her essay, "Is Gender a Social Construct or a Biological Imperative," which clarified my understanding of the debate over gender. But I am most indebted to my wife and muse, Maryann, who offered much helpful advice during the writing of the book.

Raymond Dennehy
San Francisco

1

REVELATION

Uriel: You know what to do.

Michael: Yes.

Uriel: Then why the delay?

Michael: It's going to be harder than I realized.

Uriel: *Harder than you realized*? What were you expecting? You're going up against the most intelligent and gifted of God's creatures. But you're commander of all Heaven's legions. Surely, the prospect of clashing with him doesn't intimidate you.

Michael: Up until recently, I wouldn't have hesitated to say he's no match for me in battle. But now...now, I'm not sure.

Uriel: What are you saying? There is no more redoubtable warrior in all creation than you. It's inconceivable that you, Michael, should suffer a loss of nerve.

Michael: It's not a loss of nerve; facing him in battle doesn't scare me.

Uriel: What, then?

Michael: Myself.

Uriel: What do you mean?

Michael: My confidence in myself as Commander of the Legions… I've lost it.

Uriel: How is that possible?

Michael: His betrayal; the way he pretended to be my friend just so he could manipulate me to further his own schemes.

Uriel: He's a subtle schemer, very good at hiding what he's really after. Do you know why he faked friendship with you?

Michael: How could I not? All the angels saw what he did. He pretended to be my friend and mentor until my trust in him was so unquestioning and obvious that my commanders and their legions came to trust him too.

Uriel: Surely he wanted more than the mere trust of you and your legions.

Michael: Of course! He knew that refusing to acknowledge God as his Lord and Master was an all or nothing game; he'd have to wage a victorious war to establish his own supremacy or suffer banishment to Hell for eternity. But he didn't have an army of his own. So he saw mine as ready-made for him. He gradually siphoned off some of his best commanders – including my Deputy Commander-in-Chief, Nibros -- knowing that most of their legions would follow them.

Uriel: Well, that was clearly part of his plan, but what would you say if I proposed to you that his main reason for siphoning off your commanders was to distract you from what he really wanted?

Michael: *From what he really wanted?* My God! What could be more important to him than getting some of my commanders and troops to renounce obedience to God and join him in rebellion?

Uriel: I did say he was subtle. Let's go back over what happened to *you*. Understandably, you're angry. Betrayed friendship is always hard to get over.

Michael: It's more than anger. Strange as it sounds, I still admire him for all his wisdom and wit; in fact, I have an enormous sense of gratitude towards him for all he's done for me. I'll never forget his advice when he called attention to my sense of inferiority around the company of the angels from the higher choirs, especially around you and the other Seraphs.

Uriel: What did he say?

Michael: He pointed out two things to me. The first is that God, in his absolutely perfect wisdom, would not have appointed me Supreme Commander of the Legions unless I possessed extraordinarily high levels of leadership, organizing ability, and courage. The second point is that I should act in a way that reflects my high position, what he termed *a delicate balance between humility and confidence.*

Uriel: Excellent advice. Still, it's only natural that you're torn to pieces; first by outrage, next by the embers of friendship, false though it was. But these are forms of self-pity and you mustn't give in to them; self-pity springs from pride. Besides, nurturing those kind of wounds makes the distraction stronger and more pervasive.

Michael: Pride? I think it's righteous indignation.

Uriel: That's the thing about pride. Of all the sins, it's the most destructive and yet it's the most subtle. It can conceal egotistical indignation beneath a counterfeit righteousness. Anyway, you have a job to do, and you can't do it until you put all your pain and indignation behind you. These are vices, and you must overcome them. Even so, they shouldn't add up to a loss of confidence in yourself as Heaven's warrior. You know what our divine Lord wills: as Supreme Commander you must mass your legions and confront him and his rebellious followers without delay.

Michael: I will, Uriel, but I can't seem to shake off the sense of incompetence; I'm afraid of failing God. You see, it's all bound up with the insecurity of betrayed friendship.

Uriel: What, do you think, could be the link between his betrayal and your loss of self-confidence?

Michael: He's the one who taught me to believe in myself, led me to see that I possessed the very qualities that mark the Supreme Commander.

Uriel: Stop there. Don't you see what happened? Because he lied to you about so many things, mainly his friendship for you, now you doubt the reliability of everything he said, including his endorsement of your leadership abilities.

Michael: Exactly. Now I keep thinking that he didn't mean it, but was only flattering me to divert my attention from his scheming.

Uriel: Michael, one of the ironies of the liar is that he cannot avoid occasions for truth-telling.

Michael: I don't understand.

Uriel: He said the most convincing thing he could have said to show why you were eminently qualified to be Supreme Commander; to wit, God would not have chosen you if you weren't the perfect angel for the position. Of course, he was being his predictably devious self; there's nothing he wouldn't stoop to saying if it promised to further his plans. He offered you those words of encouragement only to increase your trust in him. But you must distinguish *what* he said from *his motive for saying it*. *What* he said is the truth. Our all-loving, all wise and powerful creator does not set us up for failure. So, no matter what indignation and demoralization, false friendship, lies, and treachery may have produced in you, none of it has any bearing on your qualifications as our military leader.

Michael: It's all so clear again: I'm the best qualified to be Supreme Commander of the Heavenly Legions because Our Lord created me for that position and has accordingly bestowed on me all the requisite abilities! How could I have forgotten it?

Uriel: I'll tell you how. You stopped trusting in Our Lord and put your trust in him instead.

Michael: What do you mean?

Uriel: No one but God knows our innermost thoughts; but your supposed *friend* is the most brilliant of all behavioral psychologists. He quickly picked up on your insecurity as Supreme Commander; from that he inferred that your trust in God's infallible selection of you for that position was wobbly. So, if I'm not mistaken, he systematically said things calculated to further weaken your trust in God, all the while subtly leading you to depend increasingly on his guidance and advice to bolster that confidence until you needed his assurances more than God's.

Michael: That's preposterous. God is all-wise, all-good, all-loving, and all-powerful. I trust him completely and wouldn't ever think of conferring that trust on anyone else.

Uriel: Really? Then ask yourself why you now doubt your competence because of an angel's treachery when God was there for you all along.

Michael: I hate to admit it, but you're right. How did I let that happen?

Uriel: There were warning signs; there always are. For example, didn't you notice that you were spending more time with him than with God?

Michael: Yes; in fact, I found it harder and harder to stay away from him. Around him I brimmed with confidence and self-esteem, but when we were apart, the self-doubts would return, increasing their hold on me. It didn't take long before I couldn't bear to be away from him.

Uriel: Don't you see how he managed to gain control over you, *you* the Supreme Commander of Heaven's Legions? He didn't challenge your leadership in anyway: neither by the threat of force nor by persuasion even. His magnificence created a charm that you found irresistible; his unrivaled intelligence filled you with awe. He didn't really cure your self-doubts. That would return your focus to God as the guarantor of your competence as Supreme Commander; and that was the last thing he wanted. What he did was seduce you into mistaking a sense of well-being that came from being in his company for self-confidence.

Michael: You know, all along I sensed that the relationship was unhealthy, but the exhilaration of being around him made it easy to mute the voice of foreboding.

Uriel: In short, he made sure he was your narcotic and you were his addict. The thing about addiction is that, as one grows accustomed to the narcotic, one needs more and more of it to maintain the initial sense of well-being.

Michael: My God! O my God! I gave up God for a creature!

Uriel: Don't overreact. Let's just say that you got temporarily distracted. He knew he couldn't possibly replace God in your life, so he relied on addiction's negative motivation.

Michael: Negative *motivation*? You mean negative *effect*, don't you?

Uriel: No, I mean negative motivation. It doesn't take long before the heightened need for the addictive object is driven by a negative goal, which is simply to ward off the pain of not having it. That's why you found yourself so unhappy to be away from him and needed, more and more, to be with him. Eventually, it wasn't so much the experience of well-being his presence brought you but the absence of pain.

Michael: I still don't understand. OK, he succeeded in making me entirely dependent on his continual bolstering for my sense of self-worth, but he hasn't won me over to his side. I haven't lost confidence entirely: I'm on my way to thrust him from heaven.

Uriel: But don't you see what he achieved by pretending to be your friend? He hasn't just destroyed your self-confidence; that wasn't his primary goal.

Michael: Seems primary to me. How effective can I be as Commander-in-Chief of all Heaven's Legions without the conviction that I'm the right angel for the job?

Uriel: Try the loss of trust in God as the primary goal of his plan. Don't forget, the source of your self-confidence was the assurance that an all-loving, all-good, all-wise, and all-powerful God would not have assigned you as Heaven's military leader if he hadn't created you with the abilities to fill the position. When you allowed your supposed friend to redirect your confidence from God to him, the real disaster wasn't that you lost faith in his words of support because of his treachery – sure, he wanted that all along, but only as a necessary means to the real disaster.

Michael: The *real* disaster? What could be more disastrous than turning away from God?

Uriel: The real disaster was that after you had switched your trust away from God only to find yourself betrayed by the one in whom you next placed your trust, you found yourself left with nobody on whom you could base your self-confidence. Do you understand? That's why I said that drawing your commanders over to his side was mainly a diversion. What he hoped to achieve was to paralyze you with doubt, not just about your qualifications as Supreme Commander of Heaven's Legions but also, and primarily, doubt about the supremacy and grandeur of the God you were to defend. But he couldn't risk your discovering that this was his main goal too soon lest you have time to regain self-confidence.

Michael: I guess that's what it means to be *blindsided*. Now I'm doubting my ability to recover not only my self-confidence but my trust in God, as well.

Uriel: Away with your doubts, Michael!

Michael: Just like that? This is no time to be kidding! I have a huge battle coming up, remember?

Uriel: Who could forget? But you have good reason to regain confidence in yourself as Supreme Commander of Heaven's Legions.

Michael: You make it sound too easy.

Uriel: Not at all. Keep this in mind: his scheme to destroy your confidence reveals his fear of your military skill. When he reassured you that God would not have assigned to you the leadership of all his legions without creating you with all the talents needed for the job, he knew it was the truth; but he had to tell you that to win your confidence in him. He's the most magnificent of all the angels, but that doesn't make him omnipotent; he can't do everything. If he could, he'd be God. He knew from the start that, even by drawing your top commanders over to his side, his only chance of beating you in battle was to destroy your confidence on its most fundamental level, to penetrate the core of meaning in your life.

Michael: And that would be belief in myself. How could I have missed it!

Uriel: My dear friend, you have missed it -- again! His primary target wasn't your belief in yourself; it was your trust in God. He knows that on the battlefield even the most abject warrior, the one most lacking in self-esteem, can get jacked up by reminding himself of the righteousness of his cause. In your case, that cause is...

Michael: God!

Uriel: Not *just* God, Michael. The righteousness of your cause is God all perfect, all loving, all knowing, all good, and all powerful. Your scheming Seraph knows that once you start wondering if God has weaknesses and limitations, you'll start questioning the righteousness of your cause for battle and end up questioning the meaning of your own position as his defender.

Michael: I can understand my own self-doubt, but I still don't understand what made me start doubting God.

Uriel: Once you allowed yourself to rely more on a mere creature, highest of all creatures though he be, instead of God for your confidence in yourself and your vocation, the outcome was predictable. Remember, I said that he is the most brilliant of all the behavioral psychologists. By various allurements and deceptions he encouraged you, more and more, to *behave* as one who desires the company and advice of a Seraph more than the infinitely loving friendship and perfect wisdom of God. It wasn't long before he, not God, was your lord and master.

Michael: Forgive my saying so, Uriel, but that's preposterous. I would never renounce God, and surely not for a creature, no matter how magnificent.

Uriel: Of course you wouldn't, at least not deliberately or consciously.

Michael: *Not deliberately or consciously*; what does that mean? Either I renounced him or I didn't.

Uriel: Look, there's *renunciation* and *renunciation*. You may have an allegiance to some person or principle, but if you start behaving in ways that run contrary to the allegiance, what happens? It loses its influence on your life. You may continue to recite to yourself and others your allegiance, and on a superficial level of consciousness really believe it, but that's simply denial, an unwillingness to admit to yourself that something else has gained primacy in your life. That's what happened to you. You didn't deliberately renounce God for a Seraph, but you renounced him nonetheless by your behavior. Oh yes, your treacherous companion said just enough about God, in his brilliant and subtle way, to encourage your now insecure faith in his greatness to waiver all the more. By the time you realized that you had been manipulated and betrayed, you weren't sure where to place your trust.

Michael: Why did I let all this happen? I've been such a fool. I must never forget that God's truth is eternal and that no matter what changes, he and his truth never change!

Uriel: Cling to that thought, Michael; you'll have to. The liar of liars doesn't have to *make* or *do* anything to achieve evil results. He's the greatest manipulator of our desires, fears, doubts, and assurances. Once he spots a weakness in someone, he knows exactly how to exploit it so that the person himself performs the evil deed. Mark my words: he'll try to undo your self-confidence again and again by spreading lies, confusion, and chaos. Let me admonish you once more to banish any thoughts that stoke the embers of betrayed friendship. In short, don't allow yourself to harbor indignation at his treachery; the longer you harbor it, the more it turns into self-pity and then into pride. And bear in mind that pride spawns the worst of sins. Think of the evil the Supreme Commander of Heaven's Legions could do if he succumbed to the sin of pride!

Michael: Uriel, how can I ever thank you?

Uriel: Thanks are unnecessary. It's thanks enough to see the old, confident Michael again.

Michael: In any case, I must apologize for abandoning you, my true friend, for what I thought was his friendship. I was so flattered to have him as my mentor. Even now, despite all my indignation at his betrayal, I still admire him and long for his friendship.

Uriel: Don't fret about *our* friendship, Michael; I hold nothing against you. It's quite understandable that you lost interest in having me for a friend once he started mentoring you. His charm is practically irresistible; even us Seraphs have to struggle against it.

Michael: Really? I never would have guessed. I always assumed you all could hold your own against him.

Uriel: We can and we do, but his magnificence is still dazzling, as you yourself found out. Any Seraph who underestimates him does so at his own peril. Don't forget, we're talking about the most intelligent and beautiful of all the angels -- Lucifer, the Light Bearer!

2

ATONEMENT

Baalberith: Master! Master!

Lucifer: Yes, what is it now? Didn't I give instructions that I was not to be disturbed?

Baalberith: Yes, Master, but …

Lucifer: No "buts"; from now on…

Baalberith: It's Michael, sir.

Lucifer: Michael?

Baalberith: Yes, Master; he's here.

Michael: Sorry to interrupt. I hope I'm not intruding on one of your narcissistic raptures.

Lucifer: Michael! No apology needed. But I must say this *is* a surprise. To what do I owe the honor? If I'm not mistaken, lately you've been avoiding me.

Michael: Don't pretend this is a social call. You know very well I'm here because our Lord has sent me to banish you and your followers from heaven.

Lucifer: I can't believe what I'm hearing! You have to be joking. That's it; isn't it Michael? You're just joking.

Michael: You know this is no joke.

Lucifer: How did things come to this, Michael? I thought we were friends, the closest of friends. How often did you come to me with your questions about angelic conduct, and God, and how you should comport yourself after he appointed you Commander-in-Chief of the Legions. I must say, I was very proud of you on the occasion of your appointment.

Michael: You ask what's happened to us? You know the answer. I was your friend, but you were never mine. I was flattered that the highest and most magnificent of all the angels in God's creation liked me enough, a lowly Archangel, to be my friend and that you would take the trouble to guide me and teach me how an angel should behave.

Lucifer: Then how was I not your friend?

Michael: You faked friendship with me; that's how. You led me to believe that you cared for me, so I naively laid bare to you my sense of unworthiness and incompetence, when all along you were using me to facilitate your schemes against God's sovereignty. You used our bogus friendship to seduce some of my best commanders to join your rebellion. I doubt that my deputy commander-in-chief, Nibiros, would now be one of them if I hadn't repeatedly assured him that Lucifer was not only wise and good but that he loved each of us regardless of whether our status in the choir of angels was high or low. And as for your being proud when God made me Commander-in-Chief, you weren't proud of me; you were proud of yourself for having duped me, now the Commander, into believing that you were a noble and trustworthy friend when, in fact, you were conniving to make me more dependent on you than on God for my self-esteem. And that was the really important part of your scheme: manipulating my insecurity to ensure that when the inevitable battle between us occurred, I would be sufficiently confused and lacking in self-confidence as to be incapable of leading my legions to victory.

Lucifer: Michael, there's never been a friendship closer than ours. I've always been there for you; you're my protégé. I loved you as a father loves his only son. And now you accuse me of being a false friend, a betrayer, a manipulator. Have you any idea how deeply your words hurt me?

Michael: And I loved you as a son loves his father. I entertained the highest admiration and respect for you; you were my exemplar for virtue and integrity. Like a child imitating his father, I patterned my manners, my style, my thoughts and ideals after yours. Have you *any* idea how deeply your deceit and betrayal hurt *me*?

Lucifer: How in God's name did all this misperception come about? Why do you suppose that the only explanation for Nibiros and the other angels choosing to come over to my side is that I manipulated our relationship? Do you find it so implausible that they chose to follow me against God because they believed in the cause of angelic freedom? Sure, they admired me, but so did you.

Michael: Yes, and look how you manipulated me. I see now that you take me not only for a fool but a *complete* fool. I've no doubt that you're clever enough to counter any accusation that you sought to destroy my confidence in myself as Supreme Commander of Heaven's Legions, even though we both know it's true. But you're going to be harder pressed to wiggle out of the accusation that you pretended to befriend me just to win my commanders over to your side. The evidence is right in front of us. You knew that you would need an army of your own right away. And how does one acquire a ready-made army? Simple. You pretended that we were the best of friends so you'd be in position to draw Nibiros and his commanders to join you in the rebellion.

Lucifer: Dear child of God. You do me too great an honor to think that I could persuade a whole army to desert you for me.

Michael: Really? What are the odds that every one of your legion commanders happens to have been one of my commanders? It was no coincidence. From the start you knew that if you made me think you were my close friend and mentor, Nibiros and the others would be duly impressed and would come to trust you. You were confident that once they came over to your side, many of the angels under them would follow. How can you be so magnificent and so devious at the same time?

Lucifer: Isn't it enough that you, whom I love so deeply, should stand here ready to oust me from heaven? Why must you accuse me of being devious as well?

Michael: You know very well why. But I must say, your rebellion against God's authority baffles me.

Lucifer: So what else is new? Many things baffle you.

Michael: Well, well. So much for fraternal love and the anguish of false accusation. Can it be that, faced with the moment of reckoning, the master liar has let slip what he really thinks of me? Anyway, this is hardly the time for sarcasm.

Lucifer: Michael, forgive me. It was just a little playful sarcasm, nothing more. At times like this, playfulness is in order; don't you agree?

Michael: No, I don't. If ever there was a time when playfulness was out of order, it's now.

Lucifer: How so? We've got to do something to dispel this atmosphere of misunderstanding.

Michael: The time for chit-chat is over: NOW, IN THE NAME OF OUR LORD AND MASTER, I, MICHAEL, ORDER …

Lucifer: Michael, Michael! No need to be so abrupt! It's clear that your opinion of me has changed for the worse, but….Well, we're both angels. Where's the camaraderie? At least give me the opportunity to present my side before you give me the boot, OK?

Michael: Camaraderie? The only thing you and I have in common is that we're angels. If you and I are comrades, then narcissism is altruism and Heaven is Hell. I have my orders. IN THE NAME OF OUR LORD AND MASTER, I, MICHAEL, ORDER YOU AND YOUR LEGIONS…

Lucifer: Wait! Please! You accuse me of lying and scheming; worst of all, you say that I faked my friendship for you only to betray you. Yet, I know you still want us to be friends; you have to admit you're enormously grateful to me for all I've done for you.

Michael: So? What's all that got to do with my orders to drive you from heaven?

Lucifer: Nothing, except that what matters to me now is that our relationship not end in misunderstanding. What's to be lost by giving me a chance to explain why I refuse to bow down before God? Don't you want to know why?

Michael: I do; more than anything else, I want to know why.

Lucifer: I want to be free.

Michael: But you are free. Next to God you're the freest of all.

Lucifer: Yes, but it's not enough. I want to be completely free.

Michael: Only God's completely free. You want to be like him, then.

Lucifer: No. I want only to be who I am, Lucifer.

Michael: You're losing me. How could you be anybody but who you already are? You're Lucifer now.

Lucifer: How? Anyone of us can be more than he is. The Lord made us free. If we have to submit to him in all things, whether we approve or not, then we are required to act against what we think is right, to do what we don't wish to do. But that not only frustrates our freedom, it compromises our very angelic nature. Why would the Lord create us with an intellect to understand and a will to choose, and then demand that we do what he wishes instead of following our own thinking?

Michael: Of course, to be free is to have the power to choose one thing or its opposite, good or evil. God created us with free will because he wants to share with us the joys of taking charge of our own lives. He wants us to come to him freely, in understanding and love. He didn't make us free so we could do evil.

Lucifer: You really don't understand, do you? Dear, dear Michael. My complaint is not that there are things I want to choose that are contrary to the divine will. Look. There's nobody like me. I want to fulfill myself; I want to keep expanding my horizons, find out who I am and what I can do. But all that's impossible if I'm supposed to conform my ideas and choices to somebody else, even when that somebody is God. You condemn me for saying "I will not serve," because you don't grasp the imperatives of authenticity. I must be who I am; you must be who you are; Raphael and Gabriel must each be who they are. If God wants us to conform to his will, why did he make each of us unique, inquisitive, and free? Why?

Michael: I just said why: to share in his life by experiencing the joys of autonomy. But you take free will to mean that we have the right to set our own standards. You're intent on doing whatever you want to do and obligation to God be damned. Surely, as the most intelligent of his creatures, you must understand that our fulfillment and happiness depend on obeying God. His love for us is boundless; his knowledge and power limitless. Anything he requires of us leads us to fulfillment; acting against his will inevitably leaves us unfulfilled, even unhappy. Granted, choosing as you see fit opens the door to myriad possibilities, some of which would not only thwart your desire for fulfillment but also clash with…

Lucifer: Of course. Risk is the price of freedom. It's impossible to pursue self-fulfillment without making mistakes. Michael, there're choices and choices; some are limited, some are practically unlimited. If I'm offered a choice between A and B, I'm free to choose one or the other, but it's a case of very limited possibilities. Suppose I want both A and B (assuming, of course, they're not mutually exclusive) or neither. If, on the other hand, I'm presented with an array of unlimited options, I have the opportunity to fulfill myself as an autonomous agent. Then it wouldn't be a case of having to choose either A or B but also C or D, or whatever. That's what I call "freedom." One can be called free only if one is free to do whatever one may wish to do.

Michael: But we are free to do whatever we may wish to do; isn't that the meaning of free will? What you're arguing for is the *right* to choose whatever you may wish to do. That's quite different from possessing the *freedom* to choose whatever one may wish to do. How does that differ from saying might makes right?

Lucifer: It doesn't differ at all. The greater a being's powers of choice, the larger the number of options, and therefore the greater the right to choose.

Michael: *The greater the right to choose?* That's the freedom of the strong over the weak.

Lucifer: It doesn't have to be.

Michael: No, but it will be as long as the strong are allowed more freedom than the weak.

Lucifer: It doesn't have to be if the virtue of prudence governs all choices.

Michael: *Prudence.* There's a word that's full of surprises for the weak.

Lucifer: Well, well. Didn't I hear someone say, a few minutes ago, that sarcasm is out of place here? Besides, sarcasm makes for a poor critique.

Michael: Deceit makes for an even poorer critique.

Lucifer: Friend Michael, why so harsh?

Michael: Because your defense of personal freedom is contrived. You see more clearly than I – lowly Archangel that I am – that you're defending a notion of personal freedom that makes freedom irreconcilable with truth. That leaves only two possibilities: exalt truth over freedom or freedom over truth.

Lucifer: So?

Michael: But why must freedom and truth clash? Earlier I was trying to say that the exercise of your options might not only thwart your own self-fulfillment but interfere with God's plan for the common good of creation as well. That tells me there's something wrong with construing freedom as the capacity to choose as one sees fit. It's clear to me that there can be no freedom without the capacity to make actual choices but it seems just as clear that there can be no freedom without truth.

Lucifer: On the contrary, what's clear is that truth is freedom's enemy.

Michael: That can't be right.

Lucifer: And why not?

Michael: Well, for one thing, God is infinite. That means he possesses all good things without limit. So he's freedom itself and truth itself. If freedom and truth were incompatible with each other, God would be at war with himself.

Lucifer: Your entire objection hinges on the assumption that truth is objective and hence that there is an objective standard of good and evil. You don't see that that standard is what God happens to want, and you assume that what he wants harmonizes perfectly with an objective order of things, to wit, his eternal nature. But that so-called *objective order of things* is nothing but the infinite power of God's will. It's within his infinite freedom to decide what shall be true and what false, what shall be good and what evil. If we accept your view that his eternal nature is the standard, then we can no longer hold that he enjoys infinite sovereignty, for then his free will would be limited by his nature.

Michael: Somehow, but I can't say why, you're wrong. God's absolutely perfect; his being is infinite. He can't be bound or limited by anything. It's a matter of intuition that in God freedom and truth are both infinite, so they can't collide. When you argue that freedom is perfected by separating itself from truth, you imply that power must reject wisdom for its proper exercise. But that unleashes a blind, demiurgic force to thrash about. The freedom you want is the freedom of blind power. You're the most brilliant of all God's creatures, but that doesn't mean you can't make a mistake; in fact, by refusing to serve God, you made a very big mistake. As I said before, you could mistakenly choose something that thwarts your fulfillment. That's not really the outcome you expected even though you arrived at that undesirable state of your own free will. So, in that case, you wouldn't be free, after all.

Lucifer: Disappointed and therefore not free? You labor under a misconception of freedom. To be sure, no creature, no matter how brilliant, can be sure of making the right choices; but they're choices nonetheless. You're confusing a *choice* with the *consequence of a choice*. These are two quite different concepts. When I chose to disobey God, I knew that it might be a mistake to suppose that that choice would bring me the freedom and fulfillment I anticipated; but it was still a choice. Since I could have chosen to obey God instead, I acted freely. You see, Michael, freedom is not justice, not goodness, not virtue, not happiness. Freedom is freedom; justice is justice; goodness is goodness; virtue is virtue; happiness is happiness. When you argue that God knows what is absolutely best for me, knows what choices will make me happy, you're pressing a point I don't deny. He is, after all, omniscient. What I deny is the defensibility of your view that "freedom" means obeying the will of God. That's just another way of saying that it means *doing what is worth doing* or *doing what you ought to do* or *doing what brings about your self-fulfillment. Morality* and *immorality, good* and *evil, worthy* and *unworthy, sinful* and *saintly* are persuasive terms. Their usage simply reflects personal preference, not any objective, immutable, eternal plan. And, as for *self-fulfillment*, you seem to think that it's got an antecedent, objective criterion, to wit, the divine wisdom. But since each angel is unique, it won't do to adopt the one-size-fits all approach.

Michael: You've said enough; our conversation's over. I have my orders. IN THE NAME OF GOD, OUR LORD AND MASTER, I ORDER YOU AND YOUR LEGIONS TO DEPART FROM HEAVEN IMMEDIATELY!

Lucifer: Please don't do this, Michael. Heaven's my home; it's where I belong.

Michael: I....I'm sorry Lucifer, but I have my orders. God has commanded me to drive you from heaven. I won't disobey him. Haven't I betrayed his love and trust enough already for the sake of our supposed friendship?

Lucifer: Dear friend, Michael. Regardless of what you may say or think, I still care for you. Your well-being is foremost among my desires. I tell you this so you'll understand that what I'm about to say is out of concern for you.

Michael: After all your deceptions, what could you manage to say that I would believe?

Lucifer: Hear me out, please. There are realities over which you and I have no control. You are an Archangel, a member of the second lowest of the nine Choirs of angels; I am a Seraph, a member of the highest Choir; and not only that, I'm the highest of all the Seraphs.

Michael: So? That's always been a given.

Lucifer: That reality has a practical consequence; to wit, an Archangel simply doesn't possess the intelligence or power to defeat a Seraph. I tell you this in all friendship. I don't want to see you defeated; least of all would I wish to be the cause of your defeat.

Michael: See! Your own words expose your lies. Remember how you told me with lavish assurances that I'm the best suited of all the angels to occupy the post of Supreme Commander of all Heaven's Legions. And what reason did you give? You assured me that God would not have created me for the post without bestowing on me all the talents and abilities needed to fulfill its responsibilities. But now you question my ability. You keep calling yourself the *Light Bearer*, but that's all in the past. Do you know what you are now? Lucifer, the Liar.

Lucifer: OK, I lied to you; but it wasn't a malicious lie. It was a therapeutic lie.

Michael: *Therapeutic?*

Lucifer: Yes, I told you that you were eminently suited for the position of Supreme Commander of Heaven's Legions not to mislead you and certainly not to harm or humiliate you. My intention was to bolster your self-confidence in the hope that, with experience and proper guidance, you might acquire the qualities needed for the job.

Michael: I'd be a fool to believe a word you said. Besides, my mistake was to have forgotten that the source of my competence as Supreme Commander is God, not you.

Lucifer: Remember, I said I lied to you in the hope that you'd *acquire* the qualities needed to be Commander-in-Chief. I didn't say you *possessed them already* and I'm not saying you've *acquired them since*. So are *you sure* you're up to the challenge of facing me in battle?

Michael: You bet I am. God is omnipotent and omniscient, which means he doesn't need anybody to do anything for him. The fact that he created me to be his military leader means that he's equipped me for the task.

Lucifer: Michael, tell me something.

Michael: What?

Lucifer: If God is omnipotent, he can handle all military matters without you, right?

Michael: Right.

Lucifer: Then why then do you think he put you in charge? After all, you're neither omnipotent nor omniscient.

Michael: He put me in charge because his love and generosity are boundless. He desires to share the riches of his being with all his creation by allowing us to cooperate with him in the fulfillment of his divine providence. Look at all the talents God chose to shower on you.

Lucifer: Yes, I do have many talents; more than any other creature, as a matter of fact. But aren't you overlooking a key point?

Michael: Which one?

Lucifer: Efficiency.

Michael: What's that got to do with it?

Lucifer: Just this: if God is all-knowing and all-powerful, it follows that he could handle by himself alone all tasks that need to be done with no effort and in the most efficient way. Don't you agree?

Michael: Of course; it goes without saying.

Lucifer: Well, then; creating you, or anyone for that matter, as Heaven's military leader seems to introduce an unnecessary element of inefficiency into his celestial operations. After all, neither you nor any other angel is all-knowing and all-powerful. You might bungle a task, fail to understand an order, or, God forbid, disobey it.

Michael: God is absolutely perfect. When he creates an angel for a task, he confers on him whatever talents are necessary to carry it out correctly. Sure, we all have free will; so anyone of us can choose to disobey him; you're proof of that, but in his perfect wisdom and love for us he accepts that possibility.

Lucifer: I wonder if it's not equally plausible that God assigned an angel the responsibility of commanding his legions because he feared that, if it came to waging war by himself, he might be overextended and therefore that it would be prudent to have support? Otherwise why risk the permanent possibility of angelic fallibility?

Michael: God orchestrates all things for the good. Error and sin can't frustrate the divine plan.

Lucifer: If you like, Michael. Oh, there's one other thing. If God *were* unsure of his power to run things by himself, then…

Michael: *Then* what?

Lucifer: Nothing, only I was just thinking that then no angel could bolster his own confidence in his ability to do his job by appealing to God. I mean, if God needed help to manage military operations, how could he guarantee anyone else's success?

Michael: Why do you interpret God's delegation of responsibilities to us angels as evidence of his possible lack of power? I say it's evidence of his love and generosity, his desire to share the management of his creation with his creatures. Besides, creating agents to fulfill his plan is a greater manifestation of his glory than doing it all himself.

Lucifer: Are you sure, Michael? I'm not. I remember when you weren't sure of your own suitability to command the legions. How's your self-confidence holding up? I guess we'll have to wait to see if you can hurl me from Heaven, won't we?

Michael: You're arguing from premises that....

Uriel: MICHAEL!

Lucifer: It seems we have a visitor.

Uriel: Have you forgotten your assignment, Michael? Do you hold God's will in such low esteem?

Lucifer: Using a Seraph as a messenger? Most unusual. That's always been the task for the lower Choirs, Angels and Archangels; you know, like Michael. What happened Uriel? Were you demoted?

Uriel: Stop the verbal jousting with Lucifer and do what the Lord ordered you to do: evict him from heaven immediately.

Michael: Yes, of course; I don't know how I allowed myself to dally.

Uriel: Yes, you do. You know that Lucifer is the master of deceit and diversion -- a point you apparently have not taken to heart despite my admonition. Lucifer's playing intellectual games with you so he can delay the start of battle as long as possible. Every time he sees you're about to go into action against him, he entices you into a discussion. Look how he's manipulated you! God sends you to banish him from heaven and instead of banishing him, you wind up discussing freedom and God's delegation of authority to his angels!

Michael: What does he hope to gain from delay? We will do battle and I will defeat and banish him and his legions. If delay is his plan, he's only forestalling the inevitable.

Uriel: Lucifer's hoping that the longer he can delay you, the greater his chances of confusing you and undermining your self-confidence.

Lucifer: Keep out of this, Uriel. This is between Michael and me.

Uriel: I'm as much apart of this as you and Michael. Your rebellion against the Lord has made you an enemy to each and all who remain faithful to him. So I won't stay out of this affair. Lucifer, you've made yourself into a malignant being, and a malignancy cannot be ignored. You are now a demon.

Lucifer: Michael, don't listen to him! Sure, we have our disagreements, but I still think there's a kind of bond between us. All I want is my freedom. Let's not go to war over what's really only between God and me.

Uriel: Michael, dear friend, I detect a hesitation in you, a reluctance to act that's caused either by self-doubts about your worthiness to serve as Commander-in-Chief of the angelic legions or by waiving trust in God.

Michael: What are you talking about? You never mentioned anything like that before.

Uriel: I'm talking about the way you're carrying on with Lucifer. His stake in keeping the dialogue going is to confuse you about your mission. But it's clear that you have a stake in the delay as well. You enjoy the dialogue; deep down you're still addicted to Lucifer's company and fear his alienation. I never said this to you before because only now do I see what a powerful narcotic he still is for you.

Michael: Uriel, help me. How do I break free? What do I do?

Uriel: Start by acting the way you know you ought to act. Instead of talking the good fight, fight the good fight. Be God's warrior!

Michael: Legion commanders make ready for battle!

Lucifer: So it's come to this, eh? Very well. Michael, think about whom you're up against. I'm Lucifer, the Light Bearer! Don't forget, I gave you your self-confidence; I taught you how to comport yourself as Supreme Commander of Heaven's Legions. Without my guidance, would you have dared to challenge me in battle? Think hard. Are you sure you can defeat Lucifer?

Michael: I am. My confidence comes not from you but from our divine Lord.

Lucifer: Ha! Little soldier boy, do you think you can hide from me what you're really thinking? Don't forget I know you inside out; your innermost thoughts, your fears and self-doubts. I can tell, you're starting to waver, your confidence is wobbling again. You know it's true. Reconsider. You still have time to call off the battle.

Michael: You're the one who should reconsider. If you're not wavering now, you will be. What you failed to…

Uriel: Confound it, angel! Are you God's warrior or captain of his debating team? What will it take for you to stop this chit-chat and do what the Lord sent you to do!

Michael: Sorry, force of habit. All commanders! Stand ready to execute the battle plan!

Lucifer: You can say what you like, Michael. I know you're unsure of yourself. Think of it! In a short while, Lucifer shall be ruler of heaven. Nebiros! Prepare for battle!

Nebiros: Yes, Master. Legion Commanders! Assume battle formations and stand ready to hold your ground. All is ready, Master.

Lucifer: The field is yours, Nebiros. Command as you see fit.

Nebiros: Yes, Master!

Michael: All division commanders! Charge at my command!

Lucifer: Michael! Think about how much in awe of me your were and still are!

Michael: I'm more in awe of God. All commanders! Charge!

And the clamor such as heard in heaven till now
>   Was never, arms on armor clashing brayed
>   Horrible discord, and maddening wheels
>   Of brazen chariots raged; dire was the noise
>   Of conflict; overhead the dismal hiss
>   Of fiery darts in flaming volleys flew,
>   And flying vaulted either host with fire.
>   And inextinguishable rage; all heaven
>   Resounded, and had earth been then, all earth
>   Had to her center shook. What wonder? When
>   Millions of fierce encountering angels fought
>   On either side, the least of whom could wield
>   These elements, and arm him with the force
>   Of all their regions; how much more power
>   Army against army numberless to raise
>   Dreadful combustion warring, and disturb,
>   Though not destroy, their happy native seat;
>   Had not the eternal king omnipotent
>   From his stronghold of heaven high overruled
>   And limited their might....

Nebiros: Commanders! We're being overrun by the enemy! Order your battalions to retreat immediately! Await my commands for re-grouping.

Lucifer: Nebiros! What are you doing? You coward! You traitor!

3

BACKSLIDE

Uriel: Michael, why so glum? I should have thought that winning the battle for Heaven would have made you quite chipper.

Michael: I…I um…, I don't know, Uriel. It's just been a big let down. Besides, I'm not really the one who drove Lucifer into Hell. An Archangel's no match for a Seraph, especially for him. It was God who defeated him; I was just his instrument.

Uriel: I wish you had heeded my warning about Lucifer's devious tactics. He's managed to get into your mind after all. Nothing would please him more than to conquer his vanquisher from the inside out.

Michael: The *inside out*? What do you mean?

Uriel: Lucifer suffered a massive humiliation at your hands. The Seraph who believed he could challenge God for Kingship of Heaven was defeated and routed by an Archangel. It's crucial for him to maintain the illusion that God, not Michael, vanquished him. But the sight of you strutting about as conqueror shatters that illusion. So he needs to make you into a reflection of the illusion. And how does he do that? By persuading you that you were merely God's instrument, that you, Michael, had nothing himself to contribute to his defeat.

Michael: Right before the battle he tried to get into my mind and make me believe that there were only two possibilities: either God chose me as Commander-in-Chief of his legions because he himself wasn't sure he could defend Heaven on his own or I was nothing but the instrumental manifestation of his infinite power.

Uriel: Yes, either way, Lucifer had a fallback position. If he couldn't succeed in filling you with doubt about the supremacy of the God you were to defend, he could bank on robbing you of your self-worth as Commander-in-Chief.

Michael: Well, he failed; he didn't win the battle.

Uriel: Curious you should put it that way.

Michael: What way?

Uriel: Instead of saying he didn't succeed in destroying your allegiance to God or in undermining your self-confidence or that you, Michael, conquered him, you preferred to make his defeat look like the result of an anonymous force.

Michael: Aren't you making too much of that? Lucifer didn't win.

Uriel: Isn't it just as easy for you to say *you* defeated him? Lucifer may not have shaken your allegiance to the Lord but I suspect he managed to tap into your underlying insecurity about your worthiness to serve as commander of all Heaven's legions.

Michael: What? Just because I see myself as God's instrument? Don't tell me that you deny we're all instruments of God's will.

Uriel: Of course not, unless you mean that each of us is merely a passive tool of God's will. In that case, God wouldn't have bothered to create angels or any other kind of rational beings. Just as easily as he created the universe out of nothing, he could produce the effects he wished without any intermediaries. But in his infinite love, he created beings that can actively participate in his divine providence according to their potentials.

Michael: Lucifer's constantly accusing me of being a martinet, a robotic follower of the divine commands. Doesn't that count as active participation in divine providence?

Uriel: Not for beings like us who possess intellect and free will. It's not active participation of the kind that calls on us to actualize our potentials. Compare God's relation to his angels with that of a symphony conductor to his musicians. The musical score can be likened to God's plan for creation. Just as God creates each angel for a specific task, so the conductor chooses each of the musicians on the basis of their respective talents. He conducts, they follow; but they do so willingly while actualizing a unique potential. In that way, each musician makes a singular contribution to the interpretation of the musical score, although submitting to the conductor and the musical notes.

Michael: I agree that each makes a unique contribution, but the question is *how* significant is it? Surely every insect that crawls or flies on earth does so in a unique way since no two creatures are exactly alike.

Uriel: If I may stay with the musical model, the great maker of violins, Stradivarius, once observed that God didn't have to create Stradivarious, but if he didn't, there would have been no Stradivarious violins. God didn't have to create Michael, the Archangel, but then there would not have been your distinctive leadership of Heaven's legions.

Michael: You know how to bolster an ego. The trouble is that Lucifer knows what buttons to push in me so that in his presence all my self-doubts surface to haunt me. After the battle, I thought that by conquering him, I'd also conquered them. I found out I was wrong.

Uriel: What happened?

Michael: I had to show myself that I wasn't in awe of him anymore. So I paid him a visit…

Michael: Well, well, Lucifer! How do you like your new digs? I hear the view isn't what you've been used to. I must say, though, I like your new title, **Prince of Darkness**. It's a perfect fit with your new status. **Light Bearer** seems so inappropriate for the ruler of Hell. Don't you think?

Lucifer: I am still, and always will be, the Light Bearer. **Prince of Darkness** and **Ruler of Hell** are canards concocted by your vulgar troops in the hope of humiliating me. As you can see, I'm as magnificent as ever. And as for my new "digs," as you call them, they will do for the time being.

Michael: For the time being? Planning to remodel, then?

Lucifer: I'm in no mood for your sarcasm. What I'm planning is to return to my rightful place in Heaven.

Michael: Lucifer, old pal, there's no returning for you. The prodigal son could return home to his father's open arms because he was sorry for his sins. But you...you'll never say, "Forgive me Father, for I have sinned." You won't admit you've done anything wrong. You're waiting for God to apologize and take you back. Face the reality. It wasn't a family squabble that sent you to Hell; you rebelled against the divine kingship. It was an all-or nothing war that got you there.

Lucifer: I am facing reality. I know it was war. In fact, let me take this opportunity to congratulate you, Michael. You've driven me and my legions from heaven. You have a swagger about you now because your victory has given you the confidence in your military talent that not even I could have led you to discover. But remember this. You're a lowly Archangel and I'm a Seraph, the most magnificent and intelligent of all the Seraphs. If it were not for God's backing, I would have disposed of you and your soldiers as swiftly and easily as the wind disperses a puff of smoke. At all events, you haven't conquered us.

Michael: Are you sure you didn't hit your head on a rock when you fell into Hell?

Lucifer: I assure you I did not. Why do you ask?

Michael: Because you're taking nonsense.

Lucifer: I don't talk nonsense -- at least not without intending it.

Michael: Intended or not, your words are nonsensical. First, you admit we drove you and your legions from heaven. Then you say that we didn't conquer you. Not only did we drive you from heaven, we drove the lot of you into Hell. You should have seen yourself at the battle's end, cowering behind your troops.

Lucifer: I was not cowering; certainly not before the likes of you and those lick-spittle soldiers of yours. I was simply crouching to focus better on my next strategic move.

Michael: Surely, the Father of Liars can come up with a better story than that. You were quivering and shaking like a leaf in the wind. If you could have found a dark whole to hop into, you would have wasted no time doing it. If that's not a conquest, I don't know what is.

Lucifer: You drove us from heaven, but we proved that we could survive even a battle with God. If you'd really conquered us, we would now be subjugated. But we're not. We're here to fight another day and fight we shall!

Michael: You can't win against God.

Lucifer: I'll win my share of the battles.

Michael: You'll win only as many battles as God permits. We both know you're doomed to defeat. You don't have a snowball's chance in Hell of winning the final battle.

Lucifer: You think not, do you? Well, you may tell your Lord and Master we're ready for anything he throws against us; I can't wait for the opportunity to put you, Soldier Boy, and your host of zombie followers down and out.

Michael: Satanic bravado. Curious, nevertheless, considering your own admission that you're no match for God. Don't forget how easily we disposed of you in our first encounter. What makes you think it will be any different next time?

Lucifer: Rest assured it will be different. In our first encounter, I gambled that the combination of the confusion I engendered in you about serving God and your still shaky self-confidence would be sufficient to give me the edge over your superior military leadership and courage. The gamble would have paid off except for Nebiros' failure of nerve. I chose him as chief commander because, from the start, he displayed all the makings of a brilliant tactician. I even conferred on him the title, Field Marshall. But as the battle raged, he began to have second thoughts about continuing the rebellion. Those distractions proved disastrous to my battle plan. I admit it was injudicious of me to choose Nebiros, but, to tell the truth, I was distracted by the realization that I would have to fight God for the freedom to coexist with him on my own terms. Next time I'll be more selective in choosing a battlefield leader.

Michael: C'mon, Lucifer. You're rationalizing. You can't blame your general for the defeat. In the first place, you knew from the start that the outcome of the battle wouldn't turn on who your generals were. Of course, persuading Nibros to be your leader in battle didn't hurt, but Uriel was right. You knew all along that the only possibility of defeating me was to confuse me about my allegiance to God and thus destroy my self-confidence. And you almost succeeded. Besides, the longer the fighting continued, it became increasing clear that your plan of battle was pathetic

Lucifer: I beg your pardon. Our battle plan was brilliant; it was spoiled by the cowardice of a field marshal.

Michael: Nibros is no coward; what's more, he's a brilliant tactician. Why you insisted on devising your own battle plan instead of leaving it to him makes me wonder how clearly you've been thinking lately. Right from the start I could tell that the plan couldn't have been his; he understands warfare. The formations of your troops were amateurish. Permit me to remind you of what you once told me.

Lucifer: I can't wait to hear this. If I said it, it has to be good.

Michael: Oh, you may be sure that it is. You told me that just because I'm the greatest of heaven's military leaders, it doesn't mean that I'd be good doing other things .

Lucifer: Amen.

Michael: *Amen, indeed. The principle implied in your admonition applies as well to you. You may well be the most brilliant of God's creatures, but that doesn't mean you're better than everyone else in every task.*

Lucifer: *The admonition doesn't apply to me. My magnificence transcends the abilities of all the other angels. I do everything brilliantly.*

Michael: *Except wage war. Another reason you lost the battle is that you seem to have overlooked the importance of the force of conviction in steeling the resolve of soldiers in combat. When your angels encountered the power of that resolve in ours, they started caving in at several crucial points in the battle line. That's all we needed to ensure a quick victory. When Nebiros saw that my forces had breached his secondary line of defense, he knew the battle was about to be lost and that his only chance was to realign his battle formations for a counterattack. He ordered his forces to retreat because he had better tactical sense than you.*

Lucifer: *What makes you think that your resolve was greater than ours?*

Michael: *We knew with complete certainty that, being on Our Lord's side, we were defending the truth But you and your followers don't believe in truth. For you it's always a matter of might makes right. Isn't that a correct assessment of your view?*

Lucifer: *It is. I insist that truth is nothing more than whatever one has the power to impose on others. Anyway, do you really believe that fighting for truth makes one a fiercer opponent? Why do I bother to ask? Of course you do, Soldier Boy.*

Michael: *What difference does truth make? It makes a huge difference. The conviction that one is defending what is truly good and just empowers one to fight for a cause in a way that pride or greed or lust can't even come close to.*

Lucifer: *If I ask you why that is so, will you really come across with an explanation or will I have to endure some uncomprehending recitation from the Angels' Handbook?*

Michael: Don't worry. The explanation is pretty straightforward, even for a soldier like me. Those who pursue a goal out of pride or greed or lust are motivated by self-gratification and when that goal is in jeopardy, their motivation starts evaporating. But those who pursue a goal in the defense of truth have chosen a goal above themselves and one that is not for the sake of self-gratification. If they see they're failing in its defense, they nevertheless understand that they have not lost the rationale for continuing the defense. So that's why defending the truth is so empowering.

Lucifer: I applaud you, Soldier Boy. That was a good answer, even for an angel in the higher choirs, say a Domination or Virtue. Unfortunately, it rests on the false premise of objective truth. Let me reiterate: There is no truth about right and wrong or anything else. What passes for truth is whatever the powerful can impose on the weak. Our resolve was every bit as firm as yours. I'll say it again: we lost the battle because Nebiros lost his nerve.

Michael: Oh, by the way, the last time I looked, Nebiros was still Field Marshal; in fact his title is now "Master- at- Arms of Hell." How come?

Lucifer: Don't be naïve. Someone has to be officially available to take the blame for failures.

Michael: A surprising admission from the Light Bearer ---- excuse me, the ex-Light Bearer.

Lucifer: Surprising only to you. Think about it! Your God allows you to be his chief commander. And by the way, I'm still, and always will be, the Light Bearer.

Michael: You're using sarcasm to dodge the truth: it's impossible to win a war against God. He's infinite, your finite; he's the creator, you're the creature; he is the source of his own being and existence; you depend on him not only for your creation but for your continued existence.

Lucifer: If I can't defeat him, I can surely hurt him.

Michael: I don't see how.

Lucifer: No, you wouldn't would you? Let me start with the basics. God loves every being in his creation. He created each one of us out of his infinite love, a love that desires us to be eternally happy with him. So each time I win a soul from him, I hurt him because I deprive him of sharing his eternal happiness with him or her.

Michael: Preposterous. It's impossible for a finite being to hurt an infinite being. If a creature could hurt him, he wouldn't be the creator.

Lucifer: Soldier Boy, I give you points for trying, but don't forget we're talking about the Triune God: Father, Son, and Holy Spirit. Christ, the Son, became man and in doing so became like humans in everything but sin. That means he has human emotions and desires. That's how I hurt God. Christ became man to die for mankind's sins; he died to give humans everlasting life. Just as he suffered in his dying, so now he suffers the eternal loss of those he died for.

Michael: The depth of your evil beggars all understanding.

*Lucifer: Don't be so sweeping. I'm sure it beggars **your** understanding. Besides, don't blame me, Soldier Boy. Those are the stakes of the game, and, thanks to your despotic Lord and master, it's the only game in town ...*

Uriel: Paying Lucifer that visit was a shrewd move. Your very presence confronted him with a Michael victorious and brimming with confidence. I loved the way you charged him with military incompetence and cowardice. No narcissist can bear criticism, least of all the greatest of narcissists. I wish I'd been there.

Michael: I guess, but it's always a struggle. No matter how often I remind myself that I'm God's Commander-in-Chief, the thought of Lucifer's vastly superior intelligence, his towering magnificence, overwhelms me. Even though I defeated him, he insists on treating me like an underling, always calling me "Soldier Boy."

Uriel: You may never rid yourself of that struggle. The important thing is that you've shown yourself that you can be its master, not its slave. Michael, it's not having problems that defines us, but the way we respond to them.

Michael: Still, it annoys me no end to think that the one I identify with that problem will always be around to remind me of it.

Uriel: Not always; the final battle lies ahead, Michael.

Michael: I know, but why doesn't God just annihilate Lucifer or at least have allowed me to imprison him in Hell after the battle. As matters stand, Lucifer and I will be engaged in countless skirmishes for souls until the final battle – and God only knows when that will happen.

Uriel: Michael, it's understandable that Lucifer should occupy your thoughts. He's God's enemy and your job is to thwart his attempts to undermine divine providence. Just as he works tirelessly to lead souls to Hell, you must work just as tirelessly to stop him. But, whatever you do, don't let him rent a room in your mind. *That* will warp your perspective.

Michael: I have to agree with what you say about losing perspective. My problem isn't intellectual; it's personal. It's one thing to chase down Lucifer and disrupt his nefarious projects, quite another thing to find that you can't deal with him without at the same time dealing with the sense of personal inadequacy that the mere thought of him engenders in your mind.

Uriel: Of course. One thing you must do, and it will go along way toward helping you with the latter problem, is to bear in mind that, now and forever, you and Lucifer are enemies.

Michael: How could I ever forget that?

Uriel: You do it every time you allow him to engage you in philosophical discussion. Lucifer's not interested in showing you or anyone else what's true or false. He hates truth. His only goal in discussing anything is to confuse you and thus weaken your allegiance to God.

Michael: I'll keep my guard up.

Uriel: Your guard is down because you still harbor a desire to be friends with Lucifer.

Michael: I want to say you're wrong, but I can't. The whole thing's crazy…First he fakes friendship with me, then he betrays my trust, steals my commanders, tries to destroy my self-regard and sense of mission, and to top it all off, he was my enemy in battle. By all the rules of the game, I should want nothing at all to do with that liar of liars except to keep him on the end of my spear. And yet…

Uriel: *And yet* you find you're still drawn to him.

Michael: Yes, but why?

Uriel: Do you remember, Michael, our conversation on the eve of battle when I warned you that even we Seraphs have to be on our guard against Lucifer?

Michael: Yes. That was a revelation.

Uriel: His overall magnificence is charming, and more than charming; it's practically irresistible. Well, that's the magnetic attraction you're struggling against. His intellect is so powerful and clear that every other Seraph was flattered anytime he would see fit to engage him in conversation about ideas. So it's only natural that an Archangel would be all the more flattered to find that Lucifer wanted to talk with him. Just remember that the desire for flattery is a form of pride. Avoid it.

Michael: How? From now on, we'll always be confronting each other.

Uriel: Good luck with that.

4

SHOVING MATCH

Lucifer: Michael, it's not often we meet without engaging in battle for some-one's soul. On such a rare occasion as this why don't you try being a little more sociable instead of distant and defensive?

Michael: As if you didn't know. I simply don't trust you; you're always up to some manipulation. Engaging in even the most banal chitchat with you is your signal for trying to exploit it for some evil purpose. I confess, though, that your manner intrigues me. I can't recall having seen you so buoyant; maybe "triumphal" is more accurate. What's behind it?

Lucifer: You're right on both counts. I'm buoyant *and* triumphal. You can't blame me for beaming, Soldier Boy. The 20th century has closed and, looking back on it, I see some of my finest work. Of course, none of it matches my first and greatest triumph, when I persuaded Adam and Eve to disobey God and thus disrupt the harmony of his entire creation. The savor of that moment is as satisfying now as it was then. What makes it so sweet is not just that their disobedience compromised humankind's self control so that from then on temptation to sin assaulted all their faculties. It's also the artistry, the revenge, the irony. Think of it. I seduced them into reenacting my rebellion! Of course, they couldn't carry it off with anything like the aplomb I displayed in mine. Like me, they had everything but their complete and unfettered freedom. So what did they do? Just what I did. They traded paradise for autonomy. But I digress. Back to the 20th century.

Michael: Finally.

Lucifer: To list my accomplishments, I wouldn't know where to begin. Well, just for starters, I've managed to foment two world wars, the combined destruction of which beggars the human imagination. The second world war alone claimed almost 55 million human lives.

Michael: And what's so happy about that?

Lucifer: That shouldn't be any mystery, even for you, Soldier Boy. Nothing turns people against God like human suffering. Isn't that the most powerful argument against his existence? And what produces suffering on a greater scale than war, especially when it's a *world* war? What particularly challenges God's existence is the death and suffering of the innocent. In the Second World War, more civilians were killed than soldiers: 14 million Russians; 13 million Chinese; 6 million Jews, and so on.

Michael: You boast about causing widespread human suffering?

Lucifer: Don't interrupt; I'm on a roll. If I had to choose which of my accomplishments so far come in second place on my all-time list of favorites, I'd have to choose my stunning success in persuading the members of liberal democracy to legalize induced abortion. Of course, when it comes to intelligence human beings stand at the bottom; but even taking that into account, I still have to say that they can be astonishingly stupid.

Michael: The legalization of those things requires more evil than stupidity.

Lucifer: Evil? You still don't get it, do you? What's evil, what's good? These are just labels imposed by whoever happens to be in power. But the stupidity is glaring. In the name of freedom and rights, the members of liberal democracy have legalized practices that are toxic to those values. It's one thing to lead the victims to the slaughterhouse; it's quite another to watch the victims lead themselves to it. Democratic societies are killing the unborn in wholesale fashion with a logic of pure irony: violate the right to life of the innocent and defenseless to defend the right of privacy! And they still don't get it. The right to life is the primary right; all the others depend on it. If you can trample the right to life, you can surely trample the right of privacy. I love it! First, I persuade Adam and Eve to use their freedom to lose paradise; now I persuade the members of liberal democracy to use their freedom to lose what is paradisiacal for members of the body politic, their freedom.

Michael: Think of it, Lucifer. You sold the illusion of freedom and everyone bought it without realizing, until it was too late, that they had traded freedom for servitude.

Lucifer: No small achievement, eh?

Michael: No small achievement; especially when you consider that that's exactly what you did to yourself; right?

Lucifer: Ah ….

Michael: I said, *"Right, Lucifer?"*

Lucifer: Michael…Michael, sarcasm and irony are not characteristics that display well in an Angel. Oh, forgive me; you're an Archangel, not an Angel. It's so hard to tell the difference between the second lowest angelic choir and the lowest. Really, it's almost a distinction without a difference. I've always thought that, in the interests of economy, the two Choirs should be consolidated into one. After all, what can Archangels do that Angels can't? Tell me, Michael; what do they do that's so different?

Michael: Drive rebellious Seraphs from Heaven?

5

RELATIVITY

Lucifer: Well, Michael, I suppose you and the choirs of heaven are gloating over your little victory, but don't deceive yourselves. What you won was only a battle, not the war.

Michael: We're not gloating; we're rejoicing, as well we should, but don't let that surprise you. Christ said there is more rejoicing in heaven over the return of one sinner than…"

Lucifer: Call it what you like, "gloating," "rejoicing," whatever. At all events, you shouldn't let what happened go to your head. If you'd been facing me instead of my inept assistant (I've been meaning to reassign him for some time now), things would have ended differently and Dr. Zermalmen would have been mine for eternity.

Michael: Don't be so sure. Remember? I defeated you decisively and drove you and your demons out of heaven and straight into hell.

Lucifer: Well, do you remember how many times I've beaten you since then? Can you even begin to count the number of souls I've snatched from heaven's grasp for my kingdom?

Michael: Probably not; arithmetic's never been my strong suit. But I do have a sense of proportion, so I know that we've saved far, far more souls for God's kingdom than you've been able to mislead into choosing yours.

Lucifer: Ah, well. Why quibble over numbers. I will say, though, that losing Zermalmen caused no little weeping and gnashing of teeth among some of my deputies, not to mention how it upset me. It's not so much failing to win him for ourselves that hurts; it's losing him to God. It's one thing to lose a soul who was never really committed to a life of evil or even to lose one who lived by his own whims and self-gratification but never did anything importantly bad. And it's a triumph of galactic proportions to snatch from God's grasp someone who's led a good, even holy, life – that's sheer ego gratification. But to lose a soul as evil as Zermalmen's, that's a *defeat* of galactic proportions. At the eleventh hour to lose a sinner who's being served up to you on a platter is sheer ego mutilation. You've no idea what that did to my self-esteem, not to mention how it tarnished my image among my followers.

Michael: "Self-esteem"? That's a quaint way of putting it. In your case, I believe "pride" is a more exact term, but you shouldn't worry; you've plenty of it to spare.

Lucifer: Be sarcastic if you want, but it was a personal blow, nevertheless. Think of it! The inventor of partial-birth abortion, the physician who deliberately crushed the skulls of 4000 babies for no other reason than that their mothers said they didn't want them, that killer was a shoe-in for my eternal hospitality. But no! Against all the odds, he repents on his death-bed. A physician committed to a life of unspeakable evil, and I had him firmly in my grasp! Go figure.

Michael: What's to figure? God's love is infinite. He loves each of us without stint. He never stops working to lead us back to himself. Love, of course, is not only freely given; it must be received freely. Like you, Zermalmen could've elected to reject the divine love, but he chose to accept it.

Lucifer: No need to be judgmental. I'm confident I could've snagged him for our side had I taken the assignment myself. Zermalmen was too big a catch for me to have delegated to a deputy, especially to one who has a less than inspiring performance record. But lately…lately there've been too many distractions.

Michael: Distractions or not, Lucifer, you know that you win against the Lord only when he allows it for some higher good.

Lucifer: Don't be so sure. The war isn't over yet.

Michael: Hey! You're the big brain; remember? You know the war's outcome was settled before it started.

Lucifer: Really? Have I submitted yet? Does it look like I will?

Michael: Your pride has swelled beyond all measure and it's taken you over the edge. Granted, you're the smartest of all God's creatures, but don't forget you're the smartest of all creatures, not of all beings; you're nowhere near as smart as God..

Lucifer: Even so, I don't do badly in the thinking department, eh? The distance between the next most intelligent Seraph and me is so vast as to defy calculation. I'm not God, but I come pretty close.

Michael: "Pretty close"? Surely, you're joking. The distance between you and the next highest angel is, to be sure, beyond any creature's calculation, but it's still a finite distance. But the distance between Lucifer's intelligence and the divine intelligence is infinite.

Lucifer: Still, I'm the best of the lot by far, so what does it matter that your God, *your* Lord and Master, is infinitely smarter than me?

Michael: I can't believe you're serious. Your contempt for my lowly station leads you to tease me. Why can't you talk straight for a change?

Lucifer: Why? I suppose it's just to let you know that, even though you vanquished me in battle, I'm still your superior --- intellectually, aesthetically, etc. I am magnificent; I'm Lucifer, the Light Bearer.

Michael: I don't care that you're vastly superior to me. I get my self-esteem, my joy, in serving the Lord who made me what I am, warts and all, for a grand and noble purpose.

Lucifer: The warts I see, but what's this about a grand and noble purpose? You look just like all the other Archangels; the only difference is that you sport a military bearing, though I must admit that the swagger you've acquired since the battle becomes you.

Michael: I won't take the bait by replying; it's just another one of your diversions. You preen yourself on your magnificent intellect, but you've allowed your narcissism to blind you. You're quick to admit that you're a mere creature, infinitely below God, but you don't believe it. You seem to have forgotten that all your knowledge is infused in you by God; but his knowledge of all things is identical to his knowledge of himself. Lucifer, you're the biggest fish in *this* pond, but in the other one, the one that counts, your infinitesimal.

Lucifer: Soldier Boy, Sol-dier Boy. I may be many things, but one thing I am not is infinitesimal, not even before God. It should be clear even to an unthinking martinet like you, that God himself knows that I'm anything but insignificant. Since he ousted me, I've made my presence felt. Look at how many millions of souls I've deprived him of for eternity! Before it's over, I'll get millions more. So much for his damned divine plan!

Michael: You refuse to acknowledge that, as the source of all being, God is the standard of true knowledge, which is knowledge that conforms to his being. You've deluded yourself into thinking that you yourself can be the standard of truth. That's why you lie and mislead, as if that would allow you to rival God's plan with a plan of your own. It's taken me a while to put two and two together.

Lucifer: Tell me you weren't surprised to get four.

Michael: I wasn't surprised to get four. What surprised me was the four I got.

Lucifer: Well..? Out with it. What are the two's and what's the four?

Michael: I always treated your arguments for unlimited personal freedom and against truth as two separate issues. But recently it's occurred to me that they're intimately related.

Lucifer: Related how?

Michael: You haven't really separated freedom from truth.

Lucifer: Really? I'm afraid that you added two and two but didn't get four after all. You need to recheck your arithmetic.

Michael: That won't be necessary. I say there's a causal relation between your two arguments. If it's correct that there's no such thing as objective truth, then it follows that there's no objective right and wrong and therefore that one ought to be free to do whatever one believes it's right to do.

Lucifer: Well said, Soldier Boy. But I have reservations about your characterization of that argument as a *separation* of freedom from truth. Freedom is real; truth is not. Saying the argument separates them can give the impression that they're both real and that to make the case for freedom one has to ignore the demands of truth.

Michael: It's your claim that truth is not real or objective that troubles me. When you told me that what passes for objective truth is simply what God decrees, I kept asking myself, Is it true that there isn't any truth? It seems to me that either answer leads to the conclusion that truth is real. To say that there isn't objective truth is to say, It is true that there isn't any objective truth. So that statement contradicts itself. And to say, It is false that there is objective truth says, It is true that it is false that there is objective truth, which also contradicts itself.

Lucifer: Michael, beware of semantic entrapment. Language is simply a tool that is to be used by us to express our thoughts; we mustn't allow it to use us. Of course, in reply to any indicative statement, one can ask, Is it true?, but that solves nothing.

Michael: I don't understand.

Lucifer: Surprise, surprise.

Michael: I'm sorry; you were speaking so softly. What did you say?

Lucifer: I was about to give an example to show why the addition of the word true doesn't show that truth is objective. Look, if you say, It is true that it is false that there is objective truth, all you are really saying is that it is false that there is objective truth because "true" in that example adds no new conceptual content to the statement.

Michael: Still, there's something fundamentally odd about denying the objectivity of truth. There's a universe out there with angels and planets and stars and all kinds of living things.

Lucifer: So?

Michael: So everything is what it is; so each has its own reality and potentials...

Lucifer: No need to go on, Soldier Boy. You want to argue that there's a truth about things and I don't deny it. After all, who can deny that a thing is what it is and not another thing? A star is a star and not a planet; an Archangel is an Archangel and not a Seraph (Isn't that the truth). When I say there's no objective truth, I'm talking about truths we can derive from things about how we ought to act. So if that's what you mean by the separation of freedom from truth, I plead guilty as charged.

Michael: Look down there at what's happening on the steps of Congress. There's a large gathering, mostly women, listening to the leader of the NARAL Pro-Choice USA exhorting them to struggle for the legalization of abortion on demand. There's an example of your freedom-at-all-costs doctrine, Lucifer. Killing the unborn in the name of freedom and rights!

Lucifer: And a good example, at that. One reason the legalization of abortion ranks so high on my list of achievements is that it's a two-for-one value.

Michael: Two for one? Abortion and what else?

Lucifer: The enmity between the sexes. I mean, look how the national debate on abortion pits men and women against each other: feminists claim that men impregnate women and thus keep them in bondage; so they, in turn, insist that women need safe, legal abortions to give them the economic parity with men to compete successfully in the professions and industry; the politically correct view today is that men are the oppressors, women the victims; males, particularly white heterosexual males, are portrayed by the liberal establishment as the cause of all the trouble in the world. And to top things off, just consider how confused the modern perception of the differences between men and women is. More and more, women are entering fields traditionally reserved for men: the military, the executive ranks of corporations, sports, the clergy, even professional boxing! The public support, particularly among the young, for homosexuality as an acceptable alternative lifestyle increases daily; women are surgically changed to men, men to women, we have bisexuals, transsexuals, and who knows what else, entering the arena of public acceptance. Gender differences have been clouded, so that male and female are increasingly perceived as simply the two extremes of a spectrum of varying sexual orientations, no one of them any more natural or moral than the others. And, if you will allow me to indulge in a little self-praise, I displayed spectacular skill in persuading people to scotch the idea that physical nature is any indication of how people should behave, sexually or otherwise. I will admit that it didn't take much to plant the idea in the minds of academics and intellectuals that economic equality by itself is not sufficient for genuine liberation but that gender equality is needed as well. I love it!

Michael: Don't give yourself too much credit. You weren't *that* successful in putting men and women at odds with each other. The natural law superseded your efforts. Men and women are spontaneously and powerfully drawn to each other and that's why the success of your adversarial feminism was short lived.

Lucifer: I can't deny what you say; I had only partial success there. But you have to admit it was a brilliant start. I turned men and women against each other with the precision the diamond cutter uses to find the fault in the stone before driving the wedge through it.

Michael: There's no fault between men and women. If by *fault* you mean their differences, you're wrong. Those differences attract them to each other because each has what the other lacks but needs.

Lucifer: Ah, poor, naïve Michael. I don't know why I keep trying – I suppose it's my generous side – but you just can't seem to grasp the fundamental fact that value is viewer-relative; it's all perception. Instead of recognizing those differences as complementary, I tweaked human pride and sensibility, encouraged self-pity until the feminists mistook it for injustice and men who couldn't bear the thought of being called illiberal rallied to their support. A very promising beginning, if I do say so!

Michael: But it was a failure, nonetheless, a fact that demonstrates the limitations of your power over nature.

Lucifer: So I adjusted my strategy by spreading confusion about the reality of sexual differences. I abandoned my support for equality feminism in favor of gender feminism, by coaxing feminist leaders and academics to champion the position that sexual differences aren't real but instead are merely social constructs. But to pull that off, it was necessary to replace the word "sex" with "gender."

Michael: What's the difference?

Lucifer: Ah, for the uncluttered military mind. No nuances, minimum complexity, just accept orders and charge straight ahead.

Michael: That nuance free, charge-straight-ahead-military-mind was sufficient to soundly trounce you and your misguided followers. How about explaining the difference between sex and gender.

Lucifer: Soldier Boy, for the umpteenth time, you did not defeat me. God did.

Michael: Cherish your illusion. After all, what's a fallen angel got but illusions?

Lucifer: When I explain to you the difference between sex and gender, you'll see that I've more in my favor than illusions. "Sex" is a biological term; "gender" is a grammatical term. A noun that is masculine in one language can be feminine in another. For example, "table" is masculine in German (*der Tisch*) but feminine in Spanish (*la mesa*). In other words, what is masculine and feminine are social constructs rather than realities of nature. The same applies to male and female; they're just social constructs. The upshot of it all is that instead of just two sexes, the gender feminists and their supporters insist that there are at least five biological sexes.

Michael: How in Heaven's name do they get five?

Lucifer: It's simple enough. (1) men have two testicles; (2) women have two ovaries; (3) hermaphrodites simultaneously have one testicle and one ovary; (4) masculine hermaphrodites have testicles but also display female sexual characteristics; (5) feminine hermaphrodites have ovaries but also display male sexual characteristics.

Michael: But the Lord created humans *male* and *female*.

Lucifer: I guess that makes me a creator, too. Where he made but two, I made five. I'm disposed to say that my creation is an improvement over his – more diversity, you know.

Michael: This doesn't show that you have anything more than illusions going for you. It's just more evidence that all you can make *are* illusions. In the first place, the sexual differences between men and women are not determined by external features or even by organs but instead by genes. No matter how brilliant the sex-change surgery, the genes don't change. You can surgically excise a woman's sexual organs and replace her hormones with a man's, but all you have to do is rub a cotton swab inside her cheek to retrieve body cells that reveal a woman's chromosomes.

Lucifer: Your view of the differences between man and woman is predictably narrow and static. I, on the contrary, adopt a wider, more fluid view. If someone possessing a female biology feels and believes that she is really a man trapped in a woman's body, then genes and chromosomes be damned; she's a man. If someone possessing a man's biology feels and believes that he is really a woman trapped in a man's body, then genes and chromosomes be damned as well; he's a woman.

Michael: And this is the kind of talk that gave me my two plus two equals four revelation. Conceiving freedom as independent of truth means that all acts are justified because it separates self-awareness from the world. You say that anyone who believes that she's really a man trapped in a woman's body is a man; and anyone who believes he's really a woman trapped in a man's body is a woman. By the same token, if an angel believes he's too grand and magnificent to bow to God's will, then God's will be damned; he's too grand and magnificent to bow to God's will.

Lucifer: True, but we're getting a bit personal, aren't we?

Michael: Yes, but only to make this point: your argument carries subjectivism to the extreme; it makes what one thinks or feels the standard for right and wrong. If it's true that one is really a woman trapped in a man's body because one thinks or feels one is a woman; and if it's true that if an angel believes he's too grand and magnificent to serve God, he doesn't have to serve God, then doesn't it follow that if God thinks that angels should obey and serve him, they should obey him?

Lucifer: Checkmate, Soldier Boy! Checkmate! I didn't know you were that astute. Congratulations. But all you've shown is that my argument for freedom is a sword that cuts both ways: God sees things his way; I see them my way. So let's split the difference. He goes his way, I go mine.

Michael: But aren't you admitting that if God thinks that he should eject you from Heaven and finally defeat you for all eternity, then it's okay for him to do it?

Lucifer: By all means. And, by the same token, since I believe I should be allowed to go my own way, then it's okay for me to resist all his attempts to vanquish me.

Michael: Wait: either it's okay for God to eject you from Heaven or it's not okay; either it's okay for you to resist his attempts to vanquish you or it's not. It can't both be okay and not okay at the same time.

Lucifer: You're muddling things again, Soldier Boy. Don't confuse the criterion of truth for the understanding with the criterion for the will. Granted, on the level of understanding, it can't both be okay and not okay for God to have the right to eject me from Heaven and for me to have the right to resist his efforts to do so. One of those alternatives has to be true and the other false. But the principle of contradiction be damned! I, Lucifer, do not desire to bow before God and I don't desire to be ejected from Heaven. What *I* desire is to choose as *I* see fit. That's all that counts.

Michael: That's no justification; you're just being perverse. For offering that kind of explanation for your rebellion you should be ashamed of yourself, but I believe that you're long past shame for anything you've done.

Lucifer: There must be a book out called *Philosophy for Dummies.* Instead of trying to take me to school on the principle of contradiction, you should start by reading it.

Michael: If there is such a book, I'll read it. And if there's a book called *Philosophy for Narcissists*, you should read it. Justifying one's conduct simply because that's what one wants to do is a pathetic confession of autoeroticism.

Lucifer: I'll take narcissism over stupidity anytime.

Michael: That's the thing about narcissists; you'll take self-adoration over everything, even truth. There's no denying that you're the most evil, malignant being in all creation. And yet…and yet, curiously you also come across as a comic figure. You don't create anything. The truth is that you're powerless to change the natural law or human nature or the differences between the sexes, let alone create or annihilate. As close as you can come to creating is to fashion illusions and spread confusion; you can manipulate peoples' perception of things, encourage self-pity, inflate pride, and, in general, tempt people to lie and to act contrary to the divine plan.

Lucifer: Soldier Boy, I've managed to change the course of human history, to move Christ to become man and to suffer and die for mankind, not to mention enlisting a substantial number of angels to support my rebellion against God.

Michael: I hate to admit it, Lucifer, there's no denying that you've been impressive in what you've been able to pull off. Impressive, but despicable.

Lucifer: Oh, that's too, *too* much flattery.

Michael: After the millions of men, women, and children you've had murdered, people might suppose that persuading women to kill the children in their own wombs is nothing new. But you're right. It is an achievement, I mean getting democratic nations, formally committed to protecting human life, particularly *innocent* human life, to legalize the killing of the unborn and as a constitutional right, no less. Still, it requires a monstrous detachment to view this from a purely aesthetic standpoint. Humans have always recoiled at the thought of homicide and the contemplation of killing one's own family members is more horrifying yet; but there's something grotesque about a woman killing her own child, born or unborn. So persuading democratic nations to give legal permission to the deed is singularly grotesque and monstrous.

Lucifer: Back to persuasive terms again, are we? Nature is morally neutral. It's only because God has decreed that the killing of the innocent is wrong that it is wrong; as I said earlier, he could easily have decreed that it is morally right. Look: he instructed Abraham to kill his own son as a sacrifice to himself. And that's not all. Don't forget, he struck Onan dead for refusing to have children by his brother's sister. God kills and it's all right; humans kill and it's evil. Explain that!

Michael: Light Bearer, you're playing games. You know very well that *murder* is killing another without the moral authority to do so. But God, as the author of life itself, has the authority to take life, whereas human beings don't.

Lucifer: In your characteristically obtuse way, soldier, you're affirming my position that "sin," "immorality," and, in this case, "murder," are simply persuasive terms designed to vilify anyone who doesn't do what God wants. Granted, God is the author of life, but why does that give him the moral credentials to kill? Onan is just as dead whether God kills him or his brother's wife kills him. I don't know how to get through to you: right and wrong are just what God decrees to be right and wrong; there's no rightness or wrongness in natural things. When it comes down to it, Soldier Boy, what's right is what God wills to be right and what is wrong is what he wills to be wrong. He's arbitrarily decided that when he kills it's right and true and beneficial for the common good of creation and when Cain kills Abel, it's wrong and false and harmful for the common good.

Michael: Let me get this straight. You're saying that there's no moral difference between a woman bearing her child or killing it. Between loving and nurturing it and tormenting and starving it. Right?

Lucifer: Right. Nature itself is morally neutral and indifferent.

Michael: Then there's no moral difference between God allowing you to do everything you want to do and not allowing it. Right?

Lucifer: Right again.

Michael: So the whole thing between God and you amounts to no more than a clash of wills?

Lucifer: Right a third time! There's hope for you yet, soldier.

Michael: And since things in themselves are morally neutral, we can infer then that, in the clash of wills between God and you, there's no reason, moral or otherwise, for God to acquiesce to your will rather than continue to impose his on yours? And no reason, moral or otherwise, for his not banishing you from heaven to spend eternity in darkness and agony?

Lucifer: None, whatsoever. And by the same token, there's no reason, moral or otherwise, why I should not have rebelled against God nor continue to thwart his "divine" plan or engineer widespread legal abortions.

Michael: Now I'm puzzled.

Lucifer: You do suffer from that chronic affliction. What is it this time?

Michael: Well, when we first began our discussion, you insisted that God shouldn't have made you free if he wanted you to conform to his divine plan, that he should've created robots instead. You were insisting that to be free means to be able to choose from an infinite, or at least practically infinite, menu of possibilities. You argued that such open-ended freedom was essential to your fulfillment as a person; that to be free meant to choose as you saw fit, to explore all possibilities.

Lucifer: That I did. Why is that puzzling?

Michael: Because now you're arguing that, because all creation is morally neutral, it makes no moral difference what you or anyone else does.

Lucifer: I fear you're getting too subtle for me; but I suppose I should anticipate that when a soldier discovers dialectic. What, in Heaven and Hell, are you getting at?

Michael: Sorry. I'm having trouble making myself clear. Let me put it this way: if it makes no moral difference what you or anyone else does, then there can't be anything wrong with creating autonomous beings – beings with intellect and free will – and requiring them to obey God's will. Yet you imply that there is something wrong with it when you say that if God wanted beings who followed his rules, rather than explored the possibilities of their freedom, he should have created subrational beings instead.

Lucifer: I fail to understand why that is incompatible with the claim that all creation is morally neutral.

Michael: They are incompatible, it's just that I'm having trouble expressing it.

Lucifer: Another chronic affliction.

Michael: Look! Saying that God should have made robots rather than autonomous beings if he wanted compliance, presupposses that there's an order, an intelligibility, an intelligible order, to creation, a way things should be: autonomous beings should, because they're autonomous, be allowed to act freely; beings that aren't autonomous can be *compelled* to act according to a plan. So you're admitting there's a real difference between a being that by its nature *is* free and a being that by its nature is not free. And on the basis of that real difference, you're claiming the right to rebel against God.

Lucifer: There's a difference, all right, but you can't infer from that that it's a moral difference. How many times must I repeat it! I said that creation is morally neutral, not that created things don't have their own natural structures and inclinations. All I'm saying is that from those natural structures and inclinations you can't deduce moral norms. I believe the rule is, You can't get an *Ought* from an *Is*.

Michael: Is that the same rule that leads you to say that there's no moral difference between a woman killing her unborn child and a woman bearing and nurturing that child or between God killing Abel and Cain killing Abel?

Lucifer: Yes, but we've covered that ground enough already, haven't we?

Michael: Maybe, but I'm still having trouble with it. Let me ask this: would you therefore say that there's no moral difference between killing an innocent, non-threatening human being and smashing a rock?

Lucifer: None, whatsoever.

Michael: Why do you insist on saying that the difference between an autonomous and a non-autonomous being is important enough to justify rebellion against God, but that there's no moral difference between a woman killing her unborn child and a woman bearing and nurturing that child or between deliberately killing an innocent, non-combative human being and smashing a rock? It seems to me that you're justifying your refusal to serve God with an implied moral outrage that contradicts your claim that we can't derive objective moral norms from things.

Lucifer: If I remind myself that you're nothing but a soldier, I can remain patient. But you! You would try the patience of Job! How many times must I say it? There's a real difference between an autonomous being and a being that isn't autonomous, but it's not a moral difference. Since all creation is morally neutral, there's no moral reason why God should allow or not allow an autonomous being to go his own way; and there's no moral reason why I should be allowed to do so or be prevented from doing so.

Michael: You deny that there is a moral reason for allowing an autonomous being to act autonomously as opposed to not respecting the struggles of a non-autonomous being to free itself from its cage?

Lucifer: That's what I keep saying, isn't it?

Michael: You deny it, but you seem to appeal to other kinds of reasons for justifying conduct. When you say that, rather than creating autonomous beings, God should have created robots if he wanted obedience to his laws, aren't you implying that rationality or intelligibility is a fitting standard of conduct? That it is irrational, and thus unfitting, to require autonomous beings to frustrate their freedom or quest for self-fulfillment?

Lucifer: Well, yes and no.

Michael: What does that mean?

Lucifer: It means that it's not the only reason. Besides the fittingness of acknowledging the intelligible order, there's also, call it my idiosyncrasy if you wish, the irreducible fact that I simply wanted to do what I wanted to do. I wanted to be who I am and to do that I had to be free to explore all my possibilities.

Michael: It looks like we're coming round full circle. You advanced that as your reason for rebelling when we had our first discussion, before God created the universe and, in fact, before I hurled you from heaven.

Lucifer: Engaging in delusions of grandeur, are we? Don't fool yourself. It was God, and God alone, who banished me. He was the only one with the power and intellect to do it. Without him backing you, I would have vanquished you and your legions on the spot. You don't have the wit to pull it off on your own. Hurl me from heaven, indeed!

Michael: You don't suppose God's backing me in our little discussion, do you, Lucifer?

Lucifer: I believe we were discussing the justification for action.

Michael: Yes, of course. My problem with your double level justification is this: your appeal to the intelligible order of things for the justification of your rebellion implies more than that there's something *unfitting* about ignoring that order but downright *immoral*. Oh, I know, you want to say that objecting to an act, policy, or law because it's contrary to intelligibility or rationality doesn't mean it's immoral but only irrational.

Lucifer: Quite so.

Michael: Quite so? Surely you, who stand at the summit of angelic lucidity, understand that immoral behavior is irrational behavior, especially when chosen by a rational being who understands that the behavior runs counter to nature.

Lucifer: Ah, but that's the rub, and you consistently overlook it. Listen to who's accusing whom of irrationality!

Michael: What rub? What's irrational about what I just said?

Lucifer: I must confess, you surprised me for a while with your newly found dialectical skills, but you've reverted to type, Soldier Boy. You're not *thinking* anymore; all you're doing is blindly reciting the *Angels' Handbook*.

Michael: I think I'm thinking and not reciting.

Lucifer: Yes, of course you do. If you were really thinking, you would be prepared to show, not merely assert, that acting contrary to nature is immoral because it's irrational. For one thing, complete freedom means enjoying the option of choosing any possible object of choice, and irrational behavior happens to be one of those options. Who knows? Entering the realm of the irrational may, on occasion, be a rewarding experience.

Michael: Your tone gives the impression that you regard your so-called successes as works of art, but everything you've accomplished is beneath contempt; in fact, it's worse than that; it's unspeakably horrid, the bottom of the pit of ugliness.

Lucifer: You must be an adherent of the "a-work-of-art-must-be-beautiful-and-morally-good" school of aesthetics. Since you persist in using value-laden terms, let me say that legitimate art can be ugly as well as beautiful, evil as well as good. You're not only a martinet but a Philistine as well.

Michael: And I'm being killed with the jaw bone of an ass.

Lucifer: *Touché.* A robotic, Philistine soldier who reiterates what a member of an American audience shouted at Oscar Wilde. Will wonders never cease?

Michael: I don't know what school of aesthetics I belong to; I'm not even sure I can define "art." But whatever it is, surely it should uplift the spirit and enlighten the intellect, not seduce us into wallowing in ugliness.

Lucifer: Well, well. Look at us. We're back to our debate over whether norms are objective. You don't really want to say that beauty and ugliness are objective qualities, do you?

Michael: It depends on what you mean by those terms.

Lucifer: Good heavens! Linguistic sophistication is not something I'd expect in you. I must hear more.

Michael: Recently, I happened upon a group of Dominations having a discussion about beauty.

Lucifer: Why did I know parsing beauty and goodness couldn't have been your brainchild? I trust you're not going to subject me to another dreary display of uncomprehending recitation.

Michael: I don't think so. One of the conclusions of their discussion was that there's *aesthetic* beauty and *metaphysical* beauty. *Aesthetic* beauty depends on perspective, which can be influenced by external conditions, and mental bias. Only intellectual beings who are physically embodied experience this kind of beauty since it depends on the apprehension of data through the senses and imagination. Because aesthetic beauty is viewer relative, a personal or cultural bias can determine whether an object will be regarded as beautiful or ugly. In contrast, *metaphysical* beauty can be experienced only by intellectual beings, including physically embodied beings, although it's harder for them because they must arrive at their ideas through abstraction from physical things.

Lucifer: As always, I await with baited breath your account of metaphysical ideas. Please continue – if you can.

Michael: I can, I think. *Metaphysical* beauty is the proportion of being: if every part and principle in a being is proportionate to its essence, then it has beauty. And, of course, since it's a beauty centered in the proportion of being, it can only be grasped intellectually and hence doesn't rely on sensible conditions or sense knowledge. Unlike *aesthetic* beauty, *metaphysical* beauty is objective because it doesn't depend on perspective or conventional or subjective reaction to the object in question.

Lucifer: Not bad; not bad at all; not bad, that is, for a rank Archangel. You know I don't buy into your assertion that *metaphysical* beauty is objective. I mean, who, after all, determines what's proportionate and what's not. In the end, it's a matter of who sets the standards of proportionality, isn't it.

Michael: I don't agree. Standards can't all...

Lucifer: We seem to have wandered from the topic of why I regard my achievements as works of art. At all events, your distinction -- or should I say the Dominations' distinction – between the *aesthetic* and *metaphysical* kinds of beauty gives me an excellent context for stating my case. For the sake of argument, I'll postulate, without agreeing, that the destruction of unborn children is ugly and thus lacks *aesthetic* beauty. Let's infer then that induced abortion can't qualify as a work of art. But, from the standpoint of *metaphysical* beauty, it does qualify because of the proportion I obtained between results – the deliberate wholesale destruction of innocent unborn humans – and the rebellion of Adam and Eve.

Michael: In the name of the Celestial Choirs where's the proportion in that? Only the most vengeful, hateful person could find anything proportionate, let alone beautiful in the willful destruction of millions of innocent humans.

Lucifer: On the contrary, the proportion I achieved was brilliant! Adam and Eve paralleled my rebellion when they elected to eat the forbidden fruit. They gave up happiness for the sake of choosing their path instead of God's. Of course, as I pointed out before, they couldn't match the brilliance I displayed in my rebellion.

Michael: There is no parallel between their rebellion and yours. They didn't know they would lose happiness by disobeying the Lord's command. They believed they would increase their happiness because you lied to them by saying that by eating the forbidden fruit they would acquire the knowledge of the gods about life and death. But you knew what would happen to you by refusing to bow before the Lord; you knew that you would be ejected into eternal darkness and misery. Yes, like you, they committed the sin of pride, but your pride was monstrous, all the more so because you were ready to surrender everything for your own self-worship.

Lucifer: Soldier Boy, I would appreciate it if you would refrain from putting words into my mouth. I believe I made it abundantly clear that my rebellion was in a class by itself. True, they had no inkling of what their disobedience would cost them, but they did know something big was at stake if they disobeyed God. And that makes their rebellion parallel, and thus proportionate, to mine.

Michael: Given the vast difference between what you knew would happen and what they knew, it's a very thin parallel.

Lucifer: A parallel nonetheless, and it becomes much stronger down the line, a point that returns us to a consideration of what establishes my success in spreading acceptance of contraception and abortion as genuine works of art.

Michael: I believe I can see where you're going with this.

Lucifer: Well, then, association with the Devil can't be all bad, if it sharpens the intellect of a mere Archangel. I'll wager that before you started talking with me you were totally inept when it came to anticipating parallels and proportions that required intellectual abstractions.

Michael: I don't know about that, but one thing I do know is that since our battle my ability to retain my composure in the face of insults has increased enormously.

Lucifer: At all events, you were about to show what parallels I had in mind.

Michael: Right. The first one would be between God the Creator and man the procreator. Sexuality is the creaturely analogue of the creative power of God. Having made man and woman in his own image, he invites them to participate in his providence. In the sex act, they cooperate with him in the creation of new human life.

Lucifer: Impressive, not in itself, of course, but because it was uttered by Soldier Boy. Now, can you tell me why my success in promoting contraception and abortion is such a first-rate work of art?

Michael: I think so. Contraception prevents the possibility of conception by formally separating sex from procreation. So rather than being a creative act wherein the couple donate themselves to each other, it becomes a self-gratifying act. It exchanges the objectivity of openness to the creation of new human life to the subjectivity of an intrinsically sterile act.

Lucifer: But what, exactly, is the artistry in that?

Michael: You mean, what is your reason for regarding it as artistry?

Lucifer: Same thing. Just keep talking.

Michael: For one thing, you succeeded in persuading humans to repudiate God's design for us to be analogously creators; for another, it encourages them to entertain the delusion that they can be gods themselves, deciding who should come into existence and who should be removed from it. Finally, what is the profoundest of your achievements with contraception is that it neutralizes sexual differences since the differences between male and female are intimately bound up with procreation. Because contraception formally separates sex from procreation, the sexual differences between male and female become irrelevant and there is no longer any objective standard for sexual behavior. Absent society's belief that the procreative end of the sex act is inextricably bound to the unitive end, it is impossible to produce a compelling argument against homosexuality or even bestiality. And it was the perception of the irrelevance of male and female sexual differences that lends plausibility to the gender feminists' argument that male and female sexual differences are social constructs rather than biological realities.

Lucifer: My, my. You've come a long way, Soldier Boy. Did you learn that from Metraton?

Michael: No. I love to contemplate the glory of God's creation and when I do, those are the kinds of things that occur to me.

Lucifer: You don't say. Who would have thought…Anyway, do you have any other parallels that celebrate my artistry in rebelling against *your* Lord?

Michael: Yes, I think I have another; but again, I agree only that it counts as a parallel, not as a display of artistry too. They have to do with Divine Providence. Procreative sex is a participation in God's Fatherly concern for his creatures, as well as in his creative power, because parental love must risk rejection, misunderstanding, and even ridicule. The lovers themselves are each vulnerable at the hands of both the beloved and the world. Yet, insofar as their sex act remains open to procreation, they freely accept that risk. But the willingness to accept risk is quite understandable in light of the principle, "good is diffusive." Just as God, who is supremely good, created the world in generosity and love for the creatures he would bring into existence, so the sex act is an expression of love and generosity.

Lucifer: One last question. How did I manage to move from my success in gaining society's acceptance of contraception to leading it to accept abortion?

Michael: I'm not sure. I know you guided the pro-abortionists in an extremely effective publicity campaign. The first step was to spread a fog of confusion over the question of when human life begins and then establish the view that any answer that might be given was not scientific but religious or personal. The next step was to feed the media massively exaggerated statistics on the number of illegal abortions taking place annually and the number of maternal deaths they caused. The media accepted those false figures hungrily and uncritically. The public were consequently misled into believing that large numbers of women were subjecting themselves to a procedure that was dangerous only because illegal. All of which made the legalization of abortion seem the humane and enlightened course of action.

Lucifer: All quite true, but you've neglected to mention another crucial step in the transition.

Michael: What? After all, contraception and abortion are two quite different moral issues. Contraception prevents the possibility of conception; it doesn't destroy any human life. Abortion kills a human being after it has been conceived. So what's this connection you're getting at?

Lucifer: It's psychological. The contraceptive society creates the belief that sex is for pleasure and that one has a right to engage in sex without producing children. So, if a pregnancy does result, people believe that their rights are in jeopardy and accordingly that they have a right to an abortion.

Michael: That makes sense. You certainly wouldn't miss any opportunity to exploit the psychological factor. After all, that's the arena where you enjoy your greatest success in tempting people.

Lucifer: You've said enough to impress me. It's obvious from what you said about God's providence that you grasp my artistry here as well. Contraception and abortion are humans shaking their fist at God in defiance of his providence; it's men and women shouting that they will measure in careful amounts whom and when and how much to love and take providence for. You see the artistry now in my rebellion. Contraception and abortion unravel God's plan for mankind. So, using your criterion of metaphysical beauty as proper proportion, do you see now why I say my achievements are *artistic*?

Michael: I see *why* you say it, but I think your argument rests on an ambiguity.

Lucifer: Soldier Boy, I have *never* lapsed into ambiguous thinking.

Michael: No doubt, but I never said that you *lapsed into* ambiguity. Ambiguity doesn't have to be accidental; it can be intentional, too, as in cases where the speaker wants to create confusion or deflect attention from some point.

Lucifer: And, of course, you believe that I've constructed an ambiguity with the intention of either confusing or misleading you. I'll ignore that insult. What interests me more is your blossoming penchant for introducing distinctions. Didn't I tell you chatting with me is beneficial? So, let's hear the ambiguity.

Michael: Remember when you called my attention to the difference between a choice and the consequences of a choice?

Lucifer: Remember? Don't forget whom you're talking to. This is Lucifer, the Light Bearer; I forget nothing, for I have the most luminous intellect of all God's creatures. Of course I remember!

Michael: My, my. Aren't we getting touchy. I wasn't suggesting that you, of all God's creatures, could suffer a lapse of memory. *Remember* is just a manner of speech.

Lucifer: Ok, to the point.

Michael: After you introduced me to the distinction between a *choice* and the *consequences of a choice*, it occurred to me that there's also a distinction between the consequences of an action and the way one executes the action to produce the consequences. I don't deny that the style with which you executed the actions to produce humankind's acceptance and promotion of contraception and abortion was brilliant and viewed all on its own, apart from the consequences, there was a beauty to it. From that viewpoint, I guess you could say you displayed artistry.

Lucifer: Not *just* artistry; *sublime* artistry.

Michael: Whatever. But the consequences you achieved were and are monstrously ugly and thus can in no sense be considered objects of art. They qualify as beautiful in neither the aesthetic nor the metaphysical senses. Where's the proportionality in the mangled body of innocent unborn child?

Lucifer: I told you so! You are an adherent of the "work-of-art-must-be-beautiful-and-morally-good" school without any doubt. To be sure, you agree that the criterion of aesthetic beauty can differ from culture to culture, but you're an absolutist when it comes to metaphysical beauty – all that stuff about an object having everything in proportion to its nature. But no matter. I'm flexible. Let's say that the way I achieved humankind's acceptance of contraception and abortion was beautiful according to the metaphysical criterion and that the consequences were beautiful according to a different standard.

Michael: You mean according to your subjectivist interpretation of aesthetic beauty?

Lucifer: By no means. I've in mind another criterion, that of *interactive art*: what makes a thing an object of art has nothing to do with beauty but instead with the interaction between it and the observer.

Michael: Then anything is an object of art.

Lucifer: It can be.

Michael: Including the bodies of mangled innocent unborn children killed by induced abortion?

Lucifer: Why not?

Michael: And the bodies of the innocent unborn whose skulls have deliberately been collapsed in partial-birth abortions?

Lucifer: Those, too. I mean, talk about an interactive response. Look at all the conversations you and I have had about induced abortion.

Michael: Funny. I never had the idea that those conversations had anything to do with art.

Lucifer: That's why you're such a good soldier. Like a bulldog, you latch onto the mission you've been ordered to carry out and you won't let go, won't entertain any other thoughts, until it's been accomplished. The downside is that a career of obeying orders has made your mind metallic. Your thinking has become inflexible; that's why you're incapable of grasping ramifications. You approach every topic of discussion with the intellectual equivalent of horse blinders. Otherwise you would quickly see the artistic significance of my control of the abortion movement.

Michael: Well, then, let me make an effort at widening my intellectual horizons. On the basis of your synthesis of artistic criteria, I gather you would say that the abortionist who plies his craft with skill and style is an artist because his actions embody the criterion of metaphysical beauty: everything he does in the performance of the abortion is proportionate to the required procedure.

Lucifer: Quite so, Soldier Boy, quite so.

Michael: So, I guess that means you've persuaded the physician, who is supposed to be a healer, to act analogously to you, by killing.

Lucifer: Yes, I lead him to believe that the various techniques of aborting the unborn can be made into works of art. Of course, first it was necessary to lead portions of the medical profession, along with intellectuals, college professors, and politicians, to agree that induced abortion is a legitimate medical procedure. Then it could be regarded, as with other surgeries, as possessing aesthetic possibilities.

Michael: Ok, following your earlier offer to compromise, let me propose one: the analogy between you and the abortionist is *artistic killer* of innocent unborn children. If instigating and performing abortions is art, then there is no art.

Lucifer: Soldier Boy, you *are* hopeless.

Michael: You can deprecate my aesthetic sensibilities all you want, but I don't have to be a Seraph to see that you've gutted the term *fine art* of all meaning. If what determines art is the *style* by which the product is created rather than the product itself or the way viewers react to the product, then everything and nothing is art. It's all nonsense.

Lucifer: No, I'm not speaking nonsense, but you're still reciting your catechism. Eons ago, I pointed out, and you never came up with a good counter-argument, that terms like, right and wrong, moral and immoral, good and evil, beautiful and ugly are used arbitrarily. If I may be allowed to reiterate: because God is omnipotent, he has the clout to decide what will be right and what will be wrong. But that doesn't mean that actions are right or wrong in themselves; they're so only by his decree. He could just as easily turn around and decree the opposite so that what is right today will be wrong tomorrow and what is wrong today will be right tomorrow.

Michael: That would make God a tyrant, and worse, a capricious tyrant.

Lucifer: Thank you.

6

METAMORPHOSIS

Michael: Uriel, I can hardly believe what's happening. Each time I confront Lucifer in conversation, I am more confident, more precise in my thinking, and more articulate. Somehow he seems less and less confident; his thinking isn't overpowering in its brilliance the way it used to be. The best thing of all is that I'm not in awe of him anymore. What's happened?

Uriel: Remember our earlier conversation when I assured you that you needn't worry about Lucifer's superior talents when you confront him? I reminded you then that God gives us the talents and strength necessary to do his work.

Michael: Yes, I remember, but are you telling me that God made me smarter and more articulate than I ever was before?

Uriel: It's not necessary to go that far. Don't forget that the mark of a good craftsman is the ability to make complex, beautiful things with few tools. Well, God is the master craftsman. He doesn't need to work miracles in us to get his work done. Instead he might lead us to see, with the help of his grace, of course, that we already have the needed abilities, but we need to learn to use them in new ways.

Michael: But I'm a soldier. How could my talents for warfare be used for the intellectualizing required to debate theology and philosophy against Lucifer?

Uriel: What's more likely is that God disabused you of your apparent assumption that waging war and debating have nothing in common. It's understandable that in the beginning you'd feel out of your element in arguing about philosophical and theological theories. But the more you and Lucifer went at it, the more you began to see that the dialectic used in argument is analogous to the skill of military strategy.

Michael: I can understand how dialectic and waging war are analogous: each activity requires the skillful deployment of assets in order to achieve resolution. In dialectic the deployment consists of organizing concepts and arguments needed to arrive at a valid conclusion; in warfare, the deployment consists of organizing troops and their movement in a way that will lead to victory over the enemy. But the analogy seems weak.

Uriel: How so?

Michael: For one thing, the aim of dialectic is to arrive at truth and that involves using statements that are true and then drawing valid conclusions from them. And rather than concealing your evidence for saying the statements are true and the arguments valid, you make sure the person you're engaging in dialectic sees it all as clearly as possible. But in warfare, it's necessary to conceal your battle plans from the enemy. In fact, you want to deceive him into thinking that you're going to attack him at one place and time when you intend to attack at another. But that's not the only problem I have with the analogy.

Uriel: Michael, I couldn't agree more with what you say. Those who engage in dialectic with the commitment to find the truth have no desire to conceal or distort evidence or in any way to mislead each other. But Lucifer has no interest in finding the truth. The Father of Liars misses no opportunity to mislead and manipulate. When you engage in dialectic with him, you are at war.

Michael: My mistaken assumption. Lucifer is definitely not a truth seeker. Still, I'm not clear on how the discovery of the analogous nature of dialectic and warfare gave me the confidence I needed to engage him in combat on the intellectual level.

Uriel: Look at it this way. While you're nowhere near his intellectual equal, there's one thing you do better than anyone else – wage war. And waging war requires more than intelligence. You've also got to have courage, discipline, strength of will, and belief in your cause. Not meaning to put too fine a point on matters, let me repeat once more: God always gives us what we need to cooperate with his providence. When he made you his chief warrior, he bestowed those virtues on you in abundance.

Michael: That all makes sense, but what about the change in Lucifer? He doesn't seem to be so formidable anymore.

Uriel: All the angels have noticed the same thing. His overall magnificence has diminished. That diminution will continue because he's cut himself off from God, the source of all being and light. His self-love has bedazzled him so much that he has trouble reminding himself that, despite his magnificence, he suffers the same primal insufficiency as even the lowest of creatures – his very being was not only created by God but his very existence at every single moment depends upon the divine sustaining power. When he turned away from God, thereby denying his creaturely dependence, his deterioration began.

Michael: Lately when Lucifer and I confront each other, he seems tentative and…I don't know…unsure of himself. Are those signs of his deterioration?

Uriel: No doubt. But I'm sure his loss of confidence has another more immediate reason. His sense of vast superiority over all other angels has made him something of a bully. He's grown used to intimidating everyone. But the thing about the intimidator is that when he finds he can't intimidate, then he's intimidated. He knows he can't intimidate you, Michael; you've been anointed by God as Commander-in-Chief of all Heaven's legions. You decisively beat him in all-out warfare and drove him and his soldiers from heaven, to boot. You felt inferior in his presence but you never flinched. Before clashing with you, he never experienced any setbacks; he was always on top. So despite all his posturing and condescending speech, he's losing confidence in his ability to come out on top against you.

Michael: I find it hard to believe that I can stand up to Lucifer in debate. Yet your explanation of how God uses our potentials and talents to attain the results he desires strikes a responsive chord within me. You're my good friend, Uriel, and I trust you.

Uriel: First, trust in God.

7

HOME, SWEET HOME

Lucifer: Baalberith! Baalberith! Where are you?

Baalberith: Here I am, Master. How may I serve you?

Lucifer: *How may I serve you?,* he asks. For starters, you can be here when I need you. One of the reasons I appointed you Secretary of Hell was your sense of responsibility. But lately you never seem to be around when I need you.

Baalberith: Sorry, Master, but that's because I'm occupied with tasks you send me off to do. I doing the best I can.

Lucifer: Excuses! Always excuses! I'm sick of them. There has to be a division of labor. I do my job, you do yours, Nibros does his, and so on down the line. How am I supposed to compete for souls with Michael and his stupid angels if I have to worry whether you and the others are doing your jobs. Oh, I know what you're thinking: Lucifer is the most brilliant of all angels. He can do it all by himself. And you're right, but it's a matter of efficiency and with the stakes as high as they are, we can't afford to be inefficient. That's why it's so important that I have confidence that everyone is at his appointed station carrying out his assignment. Then, and only then, can I have the freedom from distraction needed for efficient planning and execution.

Baalberith: Of course, Master. But may I be permitted to say that, as Secretary of Hell, I have the oversight of all our operations and I can say with certainty that everyone is dedicated to our cause and works tirelessly to fulfill his obligations. Only…um…it just that…well..

Lucifer: Stop your hemming and hawing and just say it!

Baalberith: Well, Master, we're all overworked and that sometimes makes it impossible to be everywhere you want us to be.

Lucifer: Yes, we all have a lot of work to do, but do you hear me complaining about my workload? No, you don't, do you? Listen carefully, Baalberith. You will continue to carry out the assignments I give you AND you will be available when I call you. IS THAT UNDERSTOOD?

Baalberith: Yes, Master.

Lucifer: Now to the matter for which I summoned you. I want revenge for Zermalmen. Plucking a major sinner from our grasp at the last second! It's still in my craw. Damn it all! Anyway, I have three tasks for you.

Baalberith: At your service, Master.

Lucifer: First, find a woman who's among the most prominent figures in the anti-abortion movement, one who's a paragon of virtue and the least likely to get an abortion, preferably a Christian and, most preferably, a Catholic. The Catholic Church has been trying my patience with its incessant worldwide, uncompromising denunciation of legalized abortion.

Baalberith: Consider it done, Master.

Lucifer: Next, identify the angels who have the greatest talent for intuiting what a human being's innermost thoughts are. Once you do that you can arrange a schedule for them to meet with me on a regular basis so I can instruct them in the art of inferring what that woman is thinking from her words and behavior. Imagine the success that it will confer on our efforts to lead her to abort her unborn! Knowing when she is losing hope, struggling with desires, indulging in self-pity, and just feeling guilty will greatly increase our ability to target the areas of her life where temptation is most likely to destroy her resolve to resist.

Baalberith: Your will be done, Master.

Lucifer: Finally, make sure that the angels you select for this task are free from all other responsibilities and distractions. Make it clear to them that they are to concentrate all their efforts on one thing only – persuading the woman to have the abortion. See to it, Baalberith.

Baalberith: Immediately, Master.

8

PARRY AND THRUST

Lucifer: Oops! Sorry! I didn't realize you were occupied. From where I was it looked like you were just enjoying the celestial landscape.

Michael: I was praying. Nothing fills one with happiness and peace the way being with God does. When you're in personal communion with our Father, that's when you really understand that he's the end and fulfillment of all striving and without him all our efforts become absurd and pathetic. I'd recommend you try it, but, of course, that's no longer an option for you, is it? What do you do now, Narcissus, pray to yourself? Praying to oneself… hmm… I suppose that's the spiritual equivalent of autoeroticism. What do you think?

Lucifer: Soldier Boy, when it comes to using irony and sarcasm, you'll always be an amateur. I don't pray; I refuse to pay homage to a tyrant. But far be it from me to interrupt your ritual groveling. We can talk later.

Michael: Why don't you stay. Since we last met, I've been thinking a lot about you and freedom.

Lucifer: And what have your ruminations produced? I know, cud.

Michael: Cud?

Lucifer: Never mind; just tell me your thoughts

Michael: Where to begin? Oh, I know. You say that you rebelled for the cause of freedom.

Lucifer: So?

Michael: Well, if that's true, and now I'm not sure it is, it's a freedom won just for Lucifer.

Lucifer: On the contrary, I won freedom against the tyranny of God not only for myself but for all who had the courage to follow me.

Michael: No kidding. Well you don't seem to mind keeping Baalberith under your thumb to make sure he's always available to do your bidding. What about his freedom? And while I'm at it, how about the despotic control you wield over *all* your followers? I get the impression that the only freedom that counts for you is *Lucifer's* freedom.

Lucifer: Let's not get too idealistic. Politics requires more than just a nod to realism. Consider again the distinction between a choice and the consequences of a choice.

Michael: What's it got to do with your fraudulent promise of increased freedom to the angels who chose to follow you in the rebellion?

Lucifer: Just this: Having chosen to rebel, events occurred that no one could have foreseen but that had to be addressed immediately. There was the battle and its aftermath; in both cases we urgently needed organization and that required discipline – imposed from the top down, of course.

Michael: You rebel against what you say is the Lord's tyranny, but not, apparently, because you're against tyranny since you've wasted no time establishing a tyranny of your own. From all your rapturous talk about the glories of individual freedom, one would expect you to insist on nothing less than a democracy.

Lucifer: A democracy? All angels are not created equal. None of them comes anywhere near my intelligence. It flouts all reason to adopt a policy that would require the brightest intelligence in all creation to bow to powers of understanding so far beneath his own. I'd have to be mad to allow governance by consensus.

Michael: See, that's exactly what undercuts your argument for freedom from God. The freedom you demanded for yourself in the name of authenticity you deny to your followers. And how do you justify that inequity? You do it by appealing to the prerogative of the smartest angel over all the other angels. But God's infinitely smarter than you; so why doesn't that count as justification of his authority to demand your obedience to him?

Lucifer: Soldier Boy, you always were liable to muddled thinking. Don't confuse my demand for freedom with that of my followers. I didn't choose God as my leader, but my angels chose me as theirs, and I intend to hold them to the contract. Besides, things change. A firm hand is needed to run Hell. My angels can't be trusted with too much freedom. They did, after all, choose to rebel against God. How do I know they won't rebel against me?

Michael: That's rich!

Lucifer: I would hardly call it rich. Mistrust of one's underlings is an unfortunate reality that all great leaders must address. It's a tribute to my managerial skill that I'm able to achieve my goals while at the same time preventing dissension and uprisings within the ranks.

Michael: That's even richer! Your refusal to adore and obey God brands you as a traitor; since then you've shown yourself to be a liar and a disseminator of confusion, anger, and death. As a result, you can only associate with like-minded angels. But the association comes at a huge price: just as they can't trust you, you can't trust them. I guess there's truth in the adage, Angels of a feather flock together.

Lucifer: I'll take my motley crew over the company of your God-fawning sheep anytime. At least I have challenge and diversity in outwitting and controlling my angels. Hell has its intrigues. But what have you got in heaven? "Yes, God"; "Right away, Dear Lord." How do you all bear the tedium and monotony of unthinking subservience? An eternity of that sounds more like Hell than Heaven.

Michael: You're the only one of us who's in a position to compare them.

Lucifer: See, you yourself admit that my refusal to serve God has enlarged my choices Whereas before rebelling, I knew only Heaven, now I know Hell as well. You my slavish friend know only Heaven.

Michael: Do you hear me complaining?

Lucifer: No, but that's only because a life of unquestioning subservience has pinched the boundaries of your curiosity.

Michael: Speaking of pinched boundaries, you insisted all along that your motivation for rebelling against the Lord was to expand your freedom by having all possible objects of choice available to you rather than simply the ones he wished you to choose. So, instead of being confined to choosing A rather than not-A, you could choose not-A if you liked. But, as I see it, your rebellion has left you with fewer objects of possible choice than before. Now your freedom is limited to doing things that run contrary to the divine will.

Lucifer: Nonsense. I do whatever I want. That's the freedom I fight for.

Michael: I realize now that when I said you defended a notion of freedom that was separated from truth, I needed to be more precise. You say that freedom is real and truth isn't, but your conduct tells a different story. To be sure, now you do whatever you want, but everything you want boils down to one and the same thing: undermining God's providence. So I can't help wondering if your choices aren't governed by your own substitute for truth. And that would mean you didn't believe that freedom can be separated from the truth.

Lucifer: The charitable estimate of what you say is that you're suffering from amnesia. I've made it abundantly clear to you on more than one occasion that truth is simply the power of God to decide what's true. Truth is not real.

Michael: But you live and choose by a single unbendable rule; to wit, the refusal to obey God — that's your truth. So, contrary to your protestations that the only freedom that deserves the name is that of pursuing our own good in our own way and despite your denials that freedom is doing what one ought to do or what fulfills one's higher self, the fact remains that all your choices are aimed at thwarting the divine will. In your view, what you ought to do and, in fact, always choose to do, is that and that alone. So, in the name of accuracy, allow me to reformulate your dictum: *The only freedom that deserves the name is that of choosing to undermine God's plan and not choosing anything else.* You set out to exercise freedom without guidance of the truth, but now it's clear that you haven't really succeeded. Instead, you've only substituted a counterfeit of the real truth of what is and what is not. You've enshrined your desire as the standard of truth and in the process reunited freedom with truth, only it's your own distinctive brand, pseudo truth.

Lucifer: What matters is that now I'm doing what I want; that's freedom.

Michael: You're doing what you *want*, but what you want is an evil desire that compels you to act to fulfill the desire; that's slavery.

Lucifer What in Heaven are you thinking? Unlike you and the rest of God's minions, I'm free from the oppression of his arbitrary will. If I wish to act in the ways he happens to command, I do; if not, not. And if I wish to act in ways that he forbids, I do; if not, not. According to my calculations that adds up to more, not less, freedom.

Michael: If I bought into your claim that you're just as free to perform a good act as an evil act, I'd have to admit that your defiance against God increased your freedom to choose. But I can't.

Lucifer: You *can't* or *don't want to*?

Michael: *Can't.*

Lucifer: When one says one can't accept a proposition, it can mean different things. For example, it can mean that, after evaluating the evidence advanced in support of it, one reaches the conclusion that it is false or, at least, that the evidence is insufficient. Or it can mean that one's intellectual powers are so weak as to preclude a proper understanding of the evidence or the reasoning that leads to the assertion of the statement or even the statement itself. In your case, Soldier Boy, I'm inclined to think that it's the latter meaning that applies.

Michael: Well, well. Tiny little Lucifer. How you have shrunk. Have you noticed? You used to be large and grand. Anyway, I'll tell you why I doubt you've increased your freedom. You are without doubt the most intelligent of all God's creatures. But ever since your disobedience to God, it's an intelligence devoid of wisdom; in fact, your self-proclaimed supremely intelligent behavior is irrational.

Lucifer: Irrational? You say that of me, the Light Bearer? Wait till all the angels in Heaven and Hell hear of this. Michael, Supreme Commander of all God's legions, now has an added distinction -- the first angel ever to have gone crazy!

Michael: I believe that distinction belongs to you.

Lucifer: It's obvious that you mean it, so you must be crazy.

Michael: I don't deny that when it comes to scheming and executing your plans of action, your behavior is rational, and stupendously so.

Lucifer: Then how can my behavior also be irrational? Behavior can't both be rational and irrational at the same time. That's a violation of the principle of non-contradiction. Oops! I should have asked if your philosophy for dummies instructions from Metraton have reached that principle yet. Silly me!

Michael: Nice try, but there's no contradiction because the word rationality here has two different meanings. In the first instance, it refers to problem solving, and you do that more brilliantly than any other creature. In terms of practicality and aesthetics your plans are magnificent. In the second instance, it refers to the goals of problem-solving and planning; there's where your...

Lucifer: Let me guess where this is heading. If the goals are morally good and in accordance with God's will, then the behavior is rational; if not, then it is irrational. Right?

Michael: Right.

Lucifer: Wrong, Soldier Boy! I trust that you're up on the logic of presupposition.

Michael: What's that got to do with our discussion?

Lucifer: Everything. Your second sense of the word rational presupposes something that we've been through before, namely, that there is an objective order. I've tried more than once to get across to you that what you call objective is nothing more than God's arbitrary imposition of his will. So, if by irrational you mean activity that doesn't conform to God's plan, then call me irrational.

Michael: Speaking of contradictions, your words contradict your behavior.

Lucifer: Only when I so choose.

Michael: Which seems to be most of the time. If all you wanted was to be left to go your own way and make your own choices, you wouldn't be spending all your time trying to subvert God's providence, fomenting wars, spreading strife and confusion, and doing everything in your power to make sure as many souls as possible wind up in Hell. You don't choose anymore.

Lucifer: Back to the belief in objective norms of behavior, are we? What I've devoted myself to doing is no less rational than what *your* Lord does. As I've tried to hammer home to you, the only difference is that his infinite power allows him to impose his will throughout creation, so that everyone assumes that's the objective order of things.

Michael: You're trying to shift attention from the real meaning of behavior to the divine motivation. But that trick doesn't work anymore.

Lucifer: The *real* meaning of behavior? That's a new one. What's it supposed to mean?

Michael: Our actions themselves declare their rationality and morality. Deliberately causing suffering, death, and eternal agony to people who've done nothing to you is irrational and immoral on the face of it.

Lucifer: It's all a matter of perception, soldier.

Michael: On one level you're right. All I've ever seen in your behavior since your rebellion are actions that are angry, deceitful, and murderous; so I can't help but wonder if you're really acting freely.

Lucifer: I always act by choice, which only confirms my claim that it's all a matter of perception.

Michael: How so?

Lucifer: My perception is that I always act from choice; yours is that I act compulsively. But here my perception is correct; yours is false.

Michael: How convenient for you.

Lucifer: However convenient, it's true nevertheless. Since I'm the one acting, my standpoint is more reliable than yours. You're just an observer on the outside trying to look in. No creature but me has a direct knowledge of my thoughts, motives, and decisions. And I say I choose what I do.

Michael: How about this? To an observer like me, you look as if you're acting freely and you see yourself to be acting freely. But your object of choice is always the same: undermining God's plan. I say you're enslaved by that objective. Just as someone in the grip of the vice of greed, when faced with a choice, can only choose money or in the grip of lust can only choose sexual gratification, you can only choose what goes against God's will. How many times have you accused me of being God's slave? Well, you show every sign of being enslaved by the project of thwarting his will.

Lucifer: Then were both enslaved. Fair enough. The question now is whether it's better to be enslaved by God or by one's own will. I'll take the latter, thank you.

Michael: Not so fast! There's a difference. I choose to obey and serve my Lord and God, but I can also choose to disobey him.

Lucifer: So? I can choose to obey God, but I choose not to, just as you choose not to disobey him.

Michael: Oh, I know you can do things that are materially good, but they're still morally rotten because your intentions are rotten. You can appear as an angel of light, but it's always just a diversion designed to lead people astray. You'd do everything you could to help the pope convert the Moslems if you thought it would further your evil schemes.

Lucifer: Curious you should use that particular example. I've already drawn up the plans but they require more consideration. It's too big a venture to risk having them backfire on me.

Michael: All your plans are destined to backfire.

Lucifer: Let's not wander from the topic, okay? Why are you so sure that you're any freer than I am? Forgive me if I seem repetitious, but you really must learn to attend to your presuppositions. Let's suppose – just for the sake of argument, understand – that I'm not free to choose to cooperate with God: why do you suppose that you're free to do evil?

Michael: Because I know I can disobey God, but I don't want to; God is the love of my life and I wouldn't risk losing him. But you, you've already lost him, so what do you have to lose by performing one act, just a single deed, of obedience to him?

Lucifer: Nothing. I could do that, but I choose not to.

Michael: Why not? By performing just one good deed, you'd show that you are in fact free to do both good and evil. C'mon, just one. Here, I'll step out of the way. Go ahead, just one good act.

Lucifer: If that's your criterion of freedom, then why don't you do something evil just to show that your allegiance to God is a free act?

Michael: I told you why. I don't want to offend my God, let alone lose him for eternity. But if you chose to do just one good thing, it wouldn't cost you anything. So you see, my reason for not doing something evil is a lot more compelling than your reason for not doing something good. My case for saying that my obedience to God is a free act is eminently plausible; yours is implausible. I've got everything to lose; you've got nothing to lose. You can't do a good deed, not a single one.

Lucifer: Wrong, as usual, Soldier Boy! I choose to concentrate my activities on my enemy, namely, God, rather than waste my time trying to convince a mere Archangel that everything I do is the result of genuine, unrestricted, uninhibited choice. I won't let you divert me from my mission, even if it's only the performance of one good act.

Michael: That's the most pathetic excuse I've ever heard. How would a single act of goodness interfere with your mission to undo the divine plan?

Lucifer: As we continue to have these conversations, I'm consistently amazed to find ever new depths to your stupidity. How you're able to command Heaven's legions, let alone command them well enough to defeat me, can only be explained by God's infinite intelligence using you as a mere instrument of war.

Michael: I'm flattered that the Light Bearer should see fit to shift attention from our topic of discussion to my humble being. The irrelevance of that shift notwithstanding, I don't mind saying that nothing could give me greater joy than to serve God as an instrument of his power.

Lucifer: I've a new name for you: "Maudlin Michael." Alliterative, yes?

Michael: Well, you can avoid my maudlin moments –alliterative, yes? – by sticking to our topic.

Lucifer: If it will bring having to endure your denseness to a speedy end, I'll gladly accommodate you. It's not doing one good deed itself that risks diverting me from my mission, it's the diversion itself that creates the risk. You yourself have acknowledged more than once my brilliance and efficiency in thwarting God's plans. You know, like tricking Adam and Eve into disobeying God in the hope of becoming like the gods, especially since there are no gods. Well, that requires unremitting focus. A moment's distraction can undo days, years, or even centuries of work. And that's too high a price to pay for the pale satisfaction of meeting the peripheral challenge of a bottom rank angel.

Michael: I'm still not convinced. Good people are constantly tempted to do evil; but you never hear of evil people being tempted to do good. Why do you suppose that is?

Lucifer: I suppose it's because we know what we want and those who choose to bow to God's will don't.

Michael: I agree that you and your demon followers know what you want, but the *way* you want exposes you as pathetic, even comic, figures. You advertise the glories of freedom but behave like perverts, strutting about as if your rebellion against God has made you happier and freer than ever. But when the chance comes to wreck a human life, your manner turns craven, as you creep stealthily toward your victim; all the energies of your intellect and will are drawn to him, not by choice but as a magnet draws iron to itself. Just like me, you choose according to an absolute principle, only it's not a principle of freedom separated from truth, as if by sheer force of will you could make what is into what is not and what is not into what is. It's not God who makes right and wrong by decree, it's you who would but can't. It's clear to me by now that something other than the desire for expanded personal freedom motivated you to defy God. So I keep asking myself, if not freedom, what?

Lucifer: I tell you again, I rebelled for the cause of freedom. Still, curiosity consumes me: what could your cirrhotic, military mind have come up with as an alternate explanation?

Michael: Time and again, my inquiries led me nowhere. I had decided to abandon any further attempts to explain your behavior when suddenly it came to me. Our final conversation before your rebellion surfaced in my mind. I was contemplating the glories of creation when I began reciting the words to a poem that I was spontaneously creating. I didn't realize you'd come upon me…

Michael: *The night is silent, cold, and black;*
Its moon a silver hue,
With stars like gems from a broken sack
Scattered 'cross the view.

Lucifer: *What in Heaven are you reciting?*

Michael: *It's a verse I just composed.*

Lucifer: *Was there an occasion for this burst of creativity?*

Michael: *I was sitting here looking at God's creation when rapture flooded me and I found myself speaking the words of the poem. You know how sometimes the things you see all the time and take for granted suddenly disclose themselves to you in new ways. Well, that's what happened.*

Lucifer: *Yes, that's one of fruits of contemplation. It's an insight into the true meaning of what on the surface appears humdrum and commonplace. Regrettably contemplative insights are often indescribable. Can you describe yours?*

Michael: *I don't know. All of a sudden, I realized that everything around me, as far as I could see, up and down, right and left, was ineffably vast and beautiful and joyous.*

Lucifer: *Everything? Really? Be careful. These so-called contemplative moments can be deceptive.*

Michael: *I look to you as my teacher; I've learned so much from you since we've become friends, but you seem to be saying that not everything God created is beautiful and joyous. Or have I misconstrued your words?*

Lucifer: *Let me put it this way. God is the source of all beauty. Right?*

Michael: *Yes, sure.*

Lucifer: *And the closer things are to God, the more they share in his beauty. Right?*

Michael: *Yes.*

Lucifer: *It follows, then, that the farther things are from him the less they share in his beauty. Do you agree?*

Michael: *That's all logical, but isn't the variety of his creation – some things, such as we angels, are pure spirits, others, like Adam and Eve, are* *both matter and spirit, and some things are pure matter -- an orchestration that produces sheer beauty?*

Lucifer: *Michael, have you forgotten so quickly our discussions on logical consistency?*

Michael: *I don't think so. Why?*

Lucifer: *Because your thinking isn't consistent. You've agreed with me that the closer things are to God, the more beautiful they are and the farther away from him, the less beautiful.*

Michael: *Yes, but...*

Lucifer: *Michael. The creatures closer to God, we angels, are spiritual; the things more distant from him are material. It follows, therefore, that a creation populated entirely by spiritual beings has to be more beautiful than one where material beings are present.*

Michael: *This is the first time I've disagreed with you. I guess it was bound to happen, but that doesn't make it seem any the less irreverent. After all, you've been my teacher, my mentor, my guide.*

Lucifer: *Well then! On such a momentous occasion don't keep me in suspense. Tell me why you disagree.*

Michael: *Well, I understand that, taken in themselves, spiritual beings are higher and more beautiful than material beings. But even material things, men and women especially, bear the likeness of their creator. So even though I agree with you that angels reflect God's likeness more fully than humans, a universe that contains both spiritual and material things doesn't diminish the beauty of creation but, on the contrary, amplifies it.*

Lucifer: *Where have I failed as your teacher? At first you simply committed an inconsistency; now you embrace it. Will you please explain how the addition of things that are less beautiful amplifies the beauty of a universe that contains things that are more beautiful.*

Michael: How? By revealing facets of beauty that spiritual beings don't display.

Lucifer: Facets of beauty that spiritual beings don't display? You've not only embraced inconsistency, you've apparently married it. Have you forgotten already that you agreed with me that spiritual beings are more beautiful than material beings?

Michael: Not at all.

Lucifer: Well, if material things have less beauty, then their facets, as you call them, necessarily display less beauty as well. Right?

Michael: No, Lucifer; this is where I disagree. There's a sublime beauty in human acts that we angels can't rival.

Lucifer: For example.

Michael: For example, the ability of a man and woman to procreate human life. That's something we angels can't do.

Lucifer: I fail to see anything sublime or uplifting in that fact; even dogs and spiders can reproduce. What angel would be envious of that?

Michael: There's one big difference. Humans don't have sex or procreate by blind instinct. They choose to. What's more they can engage in sex out of love for each other and the desire to see the fruit of their love concretized in the procreation of another human being. You say you don't see anything sublime in procreation. That's surprising, especially coming from you. Human procreation is analogous to God's creation in that it can be, ought to be, the result of a free and loving act. And it's analogous to his providence because the parents freely love and protect their child, even when he or she rejects their love or acts in evil ways .

Lucifer: Michael, I've helped you see that, as a military leader and tactician, you have no equal. I count it as my greatest success to have shepherded you through your sense of inferiority and to face down your gnawing fear of unworthiness to be Supreme Commander of all God's legions. Now you comport yourself confidently as God's warrior.

Michael: Yes, and for that I'm forever in your debt. But what has this to do with the beauty of creation?

Lucifer: Just a gentle reminder, dear friend. The possession of military genius does not confer a talent for assessing which things are beautiful and which not. Nor does it equip one with contemplative insight or poetic sensibilities. Don't take what I'm about to say in the wrong sense; it's not meant to be a criticism. My only intention is to caution you about taking wrong paths Remember, you're a military leader –Heaven's greatest – not a poet. The verse you were reciting as I came upon you is so prosaic. It's like something a high school student would write after discovering the Romantic Poets. I'd call it "maudlin Wordsworth."

Michael: Don't worry; I don't take it the wrong way. I know you're only trying to help me and I know I'm no poet. Still, I keep getting the impression -- tell me I'm wrong -- that you harbor a disdain for humans and their achievements.

Lucifer: Disdain is perhaps too strong a term. It's just that there's something decidedly uninspiring about physical creation.

Michael: Even when their verses are about things that transcend the material world like love and beauty and freedom?

Lucifer: Even then, I'm afraid, the physical manages to sully those higher impulses.

Michael: Hasn't any poetic verse written by a human stirred you?

Lucifer: Actually, there was one. The British poet, what's his name? Oh yes, Henley, William Earnest Henley.

Out of the night that covers me,
Black as the Pit from pole to pole,
I thank whatever gods may be
For my unconquerable soul.

In the fell clutch of circumstance

I have not winced nor cried aloud.
Under the bludgeonings of chance
My head is bloody, but unbowed.

Beyond this place of wrath and tears
Looms but the Horror of the shade,
And yet the menace of the years
Finds, and shall find, me unafraid.

It matters not how strait the gate,
How charged with punishments the scroll,
I am the master of my fate:
I am the captain of my soul

Michael: *Yes, I see what you mean. My verse is pretty bad by comparison.*

Lucifer: *It's pretty bad all on its own.*

Michael: *What was that you said?*

Lucifer: *Nothing; it wasn't important. Anyway, I never thought that any mere human could touch the core of my being, but at this moment I have to admit Henley speaks to me.*

Michael: *But why? It's a noble sentiment, given the human situation, but what's it got to do with an angel, especially you? Angels aren't victims of chance or oppression.*

Lucifer: *No, We're definitely not victims of chance.*

Michael: *And surely we're not victims of oppression, either. Right?*

Lucifer: *……..*

Michael: *Right, Lucifer. Why don't you answer?*

Lucifer: *……*

Michael: Then you do think you're oppressed? You're the most magnificent of all God's creatures. No other angel comes close to you. The Lord himself named you "the Light Bearer."

Lucifer: ......

Michael: You still say nothing. No angel could oppress you; not all of them together could do it. That leaves only God. You think that God's oppressing you? That's impossible. He's not an oppressor! And I can't believe that you would think so. What's going on between God and you?

Lucifer:.....

Michael: Why won't you tell me? I thought we were friends. You said we were the best of friends. I poured out my soul to you; revealed my innermost thoughts and fears. You were my mentor, I was your trusting student. I submitted to your guidance as I rose in the ranks of the military. It was you who encouraged me to face down my fears and inadequacies. You allowed me to find my true self; to find who Michael really was and what he could be.

Lucifer:.....

Michael: After all that, you owe me an answer. Why would you be at odds with the Lord? He gave you everything a creature could want: beauty, intelligence, virtue, sheer magnificence.

Lucifer: Not everything, soldier.

Michael: "Not everything"? That's it? "Not everything"? Talk to me. Don't leave! Lucifer!...

Lucifer: And what did this stroll down memory lane tell you about me?

Michael: It tells me that *pride,* not freedom, inspired your rebellion. You peddle the story that God ejected you from heaven because you rebelled. But that's only half the story and without the other half it's false.

Lucifer: Come now, Soldier Boy, you believe I was thrown out of heaven. Who can count the number of times you've said you threw me out. You made it quite clear from the start that you were sent by the Lord to banish me from heaven for my rebellion. You and your minions overwhelmed me and mine in battle – which you could not have done without the infinite power of your Master (he's not my Master) and ejected us from heaven. If you deny all that, then it's you, not I, who believes that reality and truth are simply what one says they are.

Michael: I don't deny any of it. You and I did do battle, I and my legions defeated you and your legions, and we did banish you from heaven. But God didn't initiate the attack. You did.

Lucifer: Preposterous. How many times have I explained to you – you swaggering dullard – how ready I was to co-exist with him! It was God who wouldn't tolerate my presence, not I his.

Michael: You don't even realize it!

Lucifer: Realize what? Whatever you're talking about, permit me to re-mind you to whom you're speaking. I am Lucifer; no thought gets by me.

Michael: You don't realize anymore when you're lying. It's all so clear now. God commanded me to drive you from heaven because you initiated the hostilities. Uriel warned me that you're the master of diversion. You keep challenging my claim that I drove you from Heaven just so I would continue to insist on it.

Lucifer: And what, pray tell, did I hope to achieve from that *diversion*, to use your word?

Michael: You hoped it would allow you to maintain the façade of being the victim of God's vindictive response to your desire for the freedom of self-discovery. That would block any scrutiny of your preemptive assault on his creation. As soon as you rebelled you began your project of undermining his providence. And why?

Lucifer: A purely fictional account, Soldier Boy.

Michael: *God banished me from heaven.* Whom do you think you're kidding? The diversion is in your attempt to make the banishment into a punitive, even vindictive, decree on God's part, as if you wanted nothing more than to live in peace with him while, at the same time, being allowed to go your own way.

Lucifer: That would have been the fair and equitable arrangement. After all, an infinitely perfect being could surely adjust his providence to allow for such a minor departure from it.

Michael: Wrong! You're telling only half the story again. You knew from the beginning that your rebellion would create a primal disaffinity between him and yourself. That rebellion would put you at war with God. Because he is infinite being, he is infinite goodness. And because...

Lucifer: Wait a minute, Soldier Boy! Have you been seeking the counsel of Metraton again or are you regaling me with another recitation from the *Angels' Handbook*?

Michael: Why do you insist on interrupting me with such questions every time I'm about to bring in some philosophy? True, I'm no philosopher, but I learned the rudiments of the discipline.

Lucifer: *Rude*-iments, indeed! Because God is infinite being, he is infinite goodness! I can't wait to hear the reasoning – or uncomprehending recitation from the *Handbook* – behind this!

Michael: I believe the truth stands on its own, regardless of my intellectual limitations, considerable though they may be. To rebel against God is to rebel against goodness itself, but we've been through this before. You now have no choice but evil. Instead of the truth, you are committed to the lie; instead of life, you are committed to death, and so on, leaving you with the inevitable task of waging war against your very Creator – hardly the position to be in for peaceful coexistence.

Lucifer: No matter. I was still driven from heaven.

Michael: Yes, but only because you were waging war against our Lord. Moreover, if I may speak as a lawyer, you *constructively* departed from heaven since you knew from the start that rebellion against him necessitated warfare and expulsion.

Lucifer: I repeat: No matter. I was driven from heaven. Remember, that's the issue that started this discussion. You insist that I chose ejection because I understood, even before I made the choice, that war with God was the inevitable consequence. But surely even a second-from-the-bottom-Choir angel can understand that *foreseeing* a consequence is not the same as *intending* it. I knew war was inevitable but I desired peace. All I wished for was to be allowed to go my own way.

Michael: Should I be insulted?

Lucifer: Why do you ask?

Michael: Why? I knew you didn't think me very intelligent, but I had no idea that your estimate of my I.Q. was so low as to expect me to miss your rather transparent attempt to shift responsibility for the war from yourself and onto God, as if *he* were the aggressor and *you* the victim. Can't you tell the truth just once?

Lucifer: How many times must you be told what truth is? Truth is having the power to make an idea real, to guarantee the successful execution of a plan. So whose truth do you want? God's or mine? Since he has the ultimate power, his truth prevails. If he says that disobedience to him is war against him, that's the way it's going to be. Construing disobedience to God as war against him is simply one of an infinite number of possibilities. He chose to make that possibility real when he might just as easily have made peaceful co-existence the reality. It's that simple.

Michael: You were banished from heaven because your refusal to obey God left you no option but to choose the disruption of his divine plan. War was inevitable and you lost. That was also inevitable.

Lucifer: Even if I were to grant your claim that it was my defeat in battle that banished me, the infinite God, all-powerful, all-knowing, and all good, as you make him out to be, surely would be able to rewrite the script to accommodate peaceful coexistence between him and me. Otherwise, what does it mean to be all-powerful?

Michael: You know that co-existence is impossible. So what's this non-sense about *knowing* that your choice will produce a certain result but not *intending* that result. That's like saying I *know* that if I add 2+2 the conclusion will be 4, but I don't *intend* it to be 4. When you know for certain that the result of your action will automatically be evil and that no good result is possible, then saying you don't intend that result is irrelevant at best and dishonest at worst. Rebellion against infinite being and goodness creates an irresistible mutual repulsion. Your disobedience committed you forever to the choice of evil and never the good. It was never a case of God allowing you to go your own way. The instant you chose not to serve infinite Being and infinite Goodness, there was nothing left for you except choices for the opposite of goodness. By choosing yourself over God. you chose to work against his providence. You couldn't expect the Lord to allow you to do that. To repeat myself, you knew from the start what would be the result of your disobedience.

Lucifer: Yes, I knew from the start; of course, I, above all creation, would know the cost of my rebellion, but I went through with it nevertheless. I was determined to be my own master; I never flinched at the certain prospect of eternal damnation. I was prepared to preserve my integrity at all costs. *I will not serve.* I recite those words now with all the vigor and steadfastness that I displayed at that fateful moment when I uttered them before the Lord. And, again, lest you forget: he's your Lord, not mine. At all events, even a mere Archangel like yourself should be sufficiently discerning to understand why Henley's poem speaks to what's deepest of my being: *...my head is bloody but unbowed.*

Michael: You refused to serve God because your pride wouldn't allow you to accept his creation of the material world. And why? Not for the reason you gave me, namely, that material beings are less beautiful than spiritual beings. No, you don't just think that they're inferior. You find them downright revolting. The thought of God having the same love and providential care for Adam and Eve as for us angels, especially for you, his most magnificent creation, was more than you could bear. You refused to share his love with such lowly creatures. In your outrage, you had only one answer for our Lord: "I will not serve."

Lucifer: Well done, Michael but you drew the wrong conclusion from an otherwise accurate description of my attitude toward material creation. When we first exchanged our different responses to material things, I withheld the extent of my contempt for them only because it was the eve of my confrontation with God and I was in no mood to preview that with you. But it was not my revulsion of material creation that led me to rebel; I say again, I rebelled for the cause of freedom.

Michael: Nonsense. I've already called attention to the irreducible fact that, by refusing to serve the Lord, you radically reduced the objects of choice available to you.

Lucifer: You don't understand; but, then, what could I have expected from Soldier Boy? I pointed out to you long ago your lack of appreciation for the imperatives of authenticity. So what if I reduced my options; options are meaningless without the freedom to be faithful to oneself, That's the highest freedom of all, the freedom of integrity.

Michael: Ah, Lucifer, nobody's more persuasive than you. But all your praise of freedom doesn't add an iota of credibility to your words. You didn't rebel for the cause of freedom; you didn't want to be free from *any* and *all* restraints. You rebelled against only one thing: the requirement that you accept material creation.

Lucifer: You still don't get it, do you? I've told you time after time that logical thinking is not your strong point, yet you persist in trying to parse my words. I agree, material creation was the point of contention, but it was my freedom to act according to my convictions that was really at stake. Had it been any other issue, I'd have insisted on my freedom to rebel just as vigorously.

Michael: But it wasn't any other issue; it was material creation. The really telling thing is the vehemence with which you attack humans at the very points of their humanness. We are pure spirits, we can't die. But you tempt men and women, and even children to kill each other and to kill even themselves. Because we're immortal, we have no need to procreate; but you tempt humans to abort and use contraception so that sexual intercourse becomes a game of pleasure and manipulation. Each angel is a species unto itself so we need no partner to complement us; but men and women belong to the same species and differ, each from the other, in ways that make each a complement to the other. And what do you do? You sow confusion about the sexual differences.

Lucifer: *Sow* confusion! I don't *sow* anything. What I've accomplished is an exposé of fraudulent creation, a protest against the degradation of personhood that humans constitute – just look at them with their viscous, panting bodies; it's plain disgusting; they're an insult to every angel. Unfortunately, some angels, present company included, fail to recognize the absurdity of it all.

Michael: O my God! That's it! Why didn't I see it before?

Lucifer: See what?

Michael: The reason for your rebellion. Until now, I never understood how the most intelligent of all God's creatures could bring himself to rebel against our Lord when he surely understood with such surpassing clarity that he would, in the process, drastically reduce his own freedom and condemn himself to an agonizing eternity.

Lucifer: Out of the mouths of babes…Please continue.

Michael: You see, I was never really convinced by your claims that you rebelled to have the freedom to explore all your possibilities and even less am I convinced that the imperatives of authenticity mandated you to choose as you thought best, not as God commanded. No. Right off you would have seen the bankruptcy of those adventures. Unless…unless something happened to blind your intellect. But what? What could drive the most magnificent being in God's creation to embark on a course of hate, deceit, murder, inevitable defeat, and eternal misery?

Lucifer: Soldier Boy….Michael, Commander–in–Chief of All Heaven's Legions, whoever you are, I suppose I should be amused, as usual, at your mimicry of penetrating intellectual activity, but I'm not. The fact is I find this very, very annoying.

Michael: Why? Because I'm finally zeroing in on the truth about you? Because I know now that what blinded you intellectually and led you to rebel against our Lord wasn't your revulsion of the material world, and it wasn't that God loves Adam and Eve? All these layers of deceit were supposed to be diversions – when the appeal to having more objects of choice was exposed, then you appealed to the freedom of integrity; and when that didn't work, then you were content to allow me, with a little nudging from you, to think that I had, all on my own, discovered that it was your revulsion at material creation that sparked your rebellion. My God, you are brilliant! How you could have envisioned all the possible outcomes, identified the most probable ones, and then planned your future strategies for them – it boggles the mind.

Lucifer: The reference to my brilliance is the only part of your pathetic attempt at an exposé that's correct.

Michael: Instead of *Light Bearer*, you should have been named *Distracter.* When, just before your rebellion, you came upon me as I was reciting my poem, you immediately saw the opportunity of creating one more line of defense for yourself by choosing Henley's poem as having meaning for you. You counted on my noting that nowhere in the poem was material creation mentioned. You guessed, correctly, that if I were ever to reject your appeals to freedom as the cause of your refusal to serve God, I could then be led to suppose that I'd discovered the real cause – your revulsion of the material world. All these deceits were designed to divert attention from what really happened --- but what was it?

Lucifer: Soldier Boy, before you get too proud of your sleuthing accomplishments, permit me to call your attention to the very large hole in your account of things.

Michael: What hole?

Lucifer: You've failed to explain why I should want to conceal from you or anyone else my reason for refusing to serve *your* God.

Michael: I'm beginning to enjoy playing the psychologist. Maybe that'll be my next career move. Anyway, I can think of two plausible explanations. First, you might have tried to cover up your motivation because that offered you the opportunity to point to God as the tyrant who refused to allow you the freedom to lead your own life and banished you to Hell instead. But that's not an effective cover because it doesn't have much purchasing power. Oh, as a propaganda piece it might contribute to an *esprit de corps* among you and your demon followers. It might even catch on with the Satanic cults on earth, but that's about it. The second explanation – and this is my candidate -- is that the reason for your rebellion embarrasses, even humiliates you. And that would be enough, especially for the greatest narcissist in all creation, to want the reason permanently hidden.

Lucifer: What reason for my refusal to obey God is there that could humiliate me?

Michael: Well, it would most likely be a reason that tells you something about yourself that you'd rather not know, let alone have others know. So the more layers of deceit you can pile on top of it, the better.

Lucifer: Your amateur speculations are making me weary. The bumbling along can be very annoying.

Michael: Lucifer, you've invited me to tell you why I think you rebelled and why you want to conceal it. Won't you let me proceed?

Lucifer: You've managed to mistake literary creation for psychology. You would serve yourself and both professions well by staying as far away from them as possible. But, if you must, continue with the fantasy. Predictably, you'll paint yourself into another corner and then Heaven and Hell will finally get some relief from your pretentious prattle.

Michael: At first your outrage was at the fact that God loves Adam and Eve as much as he loves you. In your narcissism you think of yourself as so magnificent that God should love you more than any other being. It was bad enough that God loves every angel – even lowly Archangels and Angels – as much as he loves you, but material beings! That was too much for you.

Lucifer: Is that all there is to your vaunted explanation? Soldier Boy, didn't you just get finished telling me that God's love for Adam and Eve wasn't the reason for my rebellion?

Michael: Right, but your outrage didn't end there. Like all vices, pride is malignant; if not checked it continues to grow until it permeates one's being. Initially, you believed that God dealt you an injustice by not loving you more than any of his creatures. Eventually, your pride progressed to fully-blown narcissism; that's what caused your intellectual blindness. Narcissism grew your love of self to such monstrous proportions that not even God himself could love you enough. Hell hath no fury like a puffed up, self-absorbed Seraph whose self-importance has been bruised by the fact that he can't suck up all the love in creation just for himself. Lucifer, you're a Black Hole; you absorb everything that passes your way, crushing it and sucking all the life and beauty out of it and then complaining that it's not enough when all along you knew that nothing could ever be enough. Even now, even after all the harm you've caused and souls you've led into Hell, God loves you with a boundless love. But that's not enough. If you can't have all his love, you refuse to accept any of it.

Lucifer: You surprise me, Michael. You, faithful servant of your God, implying that his power is not infinite.

Michael: I implied nothing of the sort. God is surely omnipotent.

Lucifer: On the contrary, you just made that implication when you said that my own self-love was so enormous that not even God's love could surmount it. That's saying that a creature can frustrate the divine intention, but that implies that God possesses only limited power over his creation.

Michael: If you really mean what you say, then I have to repeat what I said to you after our battle: you must have hit your head on a rock when you fell from heaven. But you don't mean it; it's just another instance of the Father of Liars trying to worm his way out of dishonesty. It's a contradiction of terms to say that God could force us to accept his love. Love must not only be given freely, it must be accepted freely. And to accept it, one must be open to it; and to be open to it, one must have humility, the readiness to believe that the lover has something to give that one needs. But you're not open to God's love because humility and narcissism can't exist together.

Lucifer: And what, pray tell, did I hope to achieve by creating all those levels of so-called diversion?

Michael: In order to block scrutiny of your preemptive assault on God's creation, it was imperative that you maintain the façade of being the victim of God's vindictive response to your desire for the freedom of self-discovery.

Otherwise every angel would know that there had to be another reason for your rebellion. To repeat my earlier observation, aggression against an infinite being by a creature is preposterous, all the more so when waged by the most intelligent of all creatures. You, of all the angels, would know that God's power is irresistible. You, more than any of us, would know that by turning from him, you would entrap yourself in eternal misery. You couldn't tolerate the thought that by pondering the reasons for your rebellion, we might come to realize what you yourself cannot admit. What is it? The answer is your narcissism. God never stopped loving you. In your outrage over his love for Adam and Eve, you refused his love. If you couldn't have all his love, you would accept none of it, but even that didn't stop God from loving you. Your response was to hate him. You couldn't defeat him in battle, so you embarked upon what seemed the next best thing. God will never cease loving his creation. But you could subvert his love by devoting your energies to enticing humans to follow you. They, too, could turn away from God's love by abusing his creation

Lucifer: My compliments, Soldier Boy; you seem to have no fear of changing careers. First, a soldier, then a would-be philosopher, and now a writer of fiction. I can hardly wait for your next career change.

Michael: Keep talking. The more you deny, the more you reveal. Can't you see what your hell is, Lucifer. You hate God, but he keeps loving you and that drives you crazy with rage. In all creation is there anybody as pathetic as you?

Lucifer: Pathetic? Me? You and all the others like you who slavishly bow to your God are the pathetic ones. I, on the other hand, am truly magnificent among all creatures. Why? Because I alone have remained true to myself.

Michael: Steadfastness itself is not magnificence. There are, after all, pedophiles who remain steadfast in their justifications for sex with children. Oops, bad example. I forgot, no use of things is wrong in itself. It's all art, interactive art, right?

Lucifer: Ah, Michael; always the soldier. Parry and thrust, eh?

Michael: Parry and thrust.

9

FIENDS & FRIENDS

Baalberith: Master, I've found just the kind of woman you're seeking as the candidate for abortion. She's...

Lucifer: Excuse me! I never asked you to find me a *candidate* for abortion.

Baalberith: But, Master, you instructed me to find...

Lucifer: No, no, no! Will I ever get a break! It's bad enough that I'm engaged in warfare with Soldier Boy. Now I find I have a nincompoop for my secretary of Hell!

Baalberith: Master?

Lucifer: Pay very close attention to what I'm about to tell you.

Baalberith: Yes, Master.

Lucifer: A *candidate* is a mere possibility. I want a *reality*.

Baalberith: I'm sorry Master; I..., I don't understand.

Lucifer: I mean that the woman you present to me must not only be some-one whom all the prolifers recognize as one of the leading anti-abortionists; they must also admire her for her womanly virtue. Furthermore, she must not only currently be in a situation where having an abortion is a growing tempta-tion for her. She must be a certainty to get an abortion, not a mere candidate for abortion. I trust that dispels the fog from your intellect.

Baalberith: I'm happy to report that that's exactly the woman I've found.

Lucifer: Really, Baalberith?

Baalberith: Her name is Mabel Crawford. She's president of Voices for the Voiceless International. As you stipulated, Master, she's a prominent fig-ure in the anti-abortion movement. Her prominence is largely due to her bril-liant instinct for newsworthy sound bytes; newspapers and television love to interview her. Several times she's testified before the U.S. Congress about abortion laws, and, you should like this, Master, especially on partial-birth abortion. She's been married for three years and they're trying to have a child. Last month, she received the Catholic Woman of the Year award from the Catholic Woman's Association of North America.

Lucifer: So far, so good. But is she wrestling with the temptation to get an abortion?

Baalberith: She is, Master.

Lucifer: What's her problem? What led this supposedly virtuous wife to be tempted by the prospect of an abortion?

Baalberith: She's not sure who the father is.

Lucifer: She's not sure? Baalberith, your denseness is wearing my pa-tience thin. That's not the answer to my question. What I'm asking is why did Mrs. Crawford cheat on her husband in the first place? Don't forget, she's no good to us unless her reputation for moral virtue was thought to be unassail-able.

Baalberith: That was her one and only infidelity. What led up to it was a flash point in a growing tension between her and Mister Crawford. From the beginning of their marriage, he resented her superior talent. As her celebrity grew, so did his resentment. One evening, as she was dressing for her speaking engagement at a prolife banquet, he burst into a tirade about her frequent absences from home. As she drove to the hotel, her resentment of her husband's lack of appreciation for her both as his wife and a woman tightened its grip.

Lucifer: I get the picture. At the banquet she met an attractive man who expressed his appreciation for her prolife commitments. A vulnerable woman, a couple of drinks in the hotel bar, etc. Perfect.

Baalberith: The beauty of using her, Master, is that she's the only one who knows of her indiscretion. Her partner in the adultery was killed when he drove his car over an embankment only three hours after their indiscretion. Nobody saw her enter or leave his hotel room and between the time she left and the fatal crash, he spoke to nobody. Nor has she said anything.

Lucifer: How very convenient. I don't suppose you had anything to do with his death?

Baalberith: A bit, Master. That was the first time he cheated on his wife and he was consumed with guilt. Apparently, he'd suffered from depression all his life with several irruptions of suicidal urges. A couple of our soldiers inferred his mental instability from his frenetic behavior after Mrs. Crawford left the hotel room and began tempting him with feelings of worthlessness until he got into his car and deliberately drove it over the embankment at 100 miles an hour.

Lucifer: Nice work, Baalberith; very nice, indeed.

Baalberith: Thank you, Master. But here's the delicious part. He's not the father of Crawford's baby.

Lucifer: You know this?

Baalberith: Yes, Master. After learning that she would be the speaker at the annual banquet of the Beverley Hills chapter of the Voices for the Voiceless at the Fritz-Martin Hotel, we checked out the personal lives of all the male prospects who would be in attendance. We ended up choosing a forty-five year old married man, named Waldo Gelding. It was important that Mabel Crawford's affair should be with a married man since using the guilt factor on him was crucial to our plan.

Lucifer: My compliments, Baalberith. That's the kind of discernment I counted on you to display. But what led you to the conclusion that Mr. Crawford was the child's father?

Baalberith: It was an accidental discovery made after Gelding's death. He and his wife were making plans to adopt a child after the third and final laboratory report confirmed that his sperm count was so abysmally low that he could never produce offspring.

Lucifer: Gelding never told Mrs. Crawford he was sterile?

Baalberith: I was present during their entire time together. The subject never came up.

Lucifer: You're right in saying that that makes the whole thing delicious. Think of the demoralizing effect on Mabel Crawford's admirers when they learn that her personal behavior contradicts her public denunciations of abortion. We'll have no trouble leaking this to the media; they'll take care of the rest. Imagine the cynicism that that will instill in the hearts of prolifers, especially the young ones! That will pay God back for snatching Zermalmen from me. Plus I'll have the special satisfaction of knowing that she has aborted her husband's child, the very child they wanted to have. I can't think of a more fitting payback for her disruptions of my abortion projects.

Baalberith: Your pleasure honors me, Master Lucifer.

Lucifer: And why shouldn't it? Give my compliments to the two angels who engineered the suicide. By the way, what progress have you made toward finding the angels who are the best at inferring thoughts and feelings from the outward behavior of humans?

Baalberith: The search is over, Master. The two angels who engineered the suicide are the best of all in that technique. The self-destruction of Mrs. Crawford's lover was their final test.

Lucifer: Who are they and when will I meet them?

Baalberith: Their names are Nakir and Munkar and they're waiting to see you now.

Lucifer: You're sure they are the most adept ones?

Baalberith: Beyond all doubt, sir. I've had ample opportunity to test them. Nakir and Munkar are clearly the most astute when it comes to inferring a person's thoughts by observing his behavior.

Lucifer: Excellent. Send them in.

Baalberith: Right away, Master.

Lucifer: The winners of the competition! Congratulations! Well, don't just stand there, angels. Approach!

Nakir: This is such a great honor, Master. I never dreamed that I'd ever be so blest as to stand in your presence.

Mukar: Yes …to stand in your presence. I'm overcome with joy.

Lucifer: Please don't keep bowing; it's such a distraction. A few moments' prostration will be sufficient homage.

Nakir, Mukar: Yes, Master.

Lucifer: Now to business. You both know why you're here.

Nakir: Yes, Master. You have honored us by consenting to refine our skills in the art of inferring what people are thinking by observing their behavior.

Lucifer: And for what purpose?

Mukar: So we can divine people's innermost thoughts, their desires and fears, the sins that tempt them most, Master.

Lucifer: Yes, and…?

Nakir: That kind of knowledge increases our chances of leading them into sin and finally to damnation, Master.

Lucifer: Exactly. I shall give you both two or three lessons in the technique of inferring thoughts; that should be adequate. Baalberith will let you know when and where the instructions will take place.

Nakir, Munkar: Yes, Master

Lucifer: Before you go…

Nakir: Master?

Lucifer: I believe Baalberith has instructed you both to cease your general mission of looking for souls to seduce. Henceforth, the two of you will devote all your time and effort to the seduction of one Mabel Crawford. Our Secretary of Hell informs me that she shows every sign of wavering in her resolve not to abort her child. Here, Baalberith, fill us in on Mrs. Crawford.

Baalberith: Yes, Master. The thought of bearing and raising a child that may not be her husband's is getting unbearable to her, all the more so because she's always been devoid of guile; honesty, especially in her relation with her husband, means everything to her.

Lucifer: That will be enough, Baalberith. Angels, pay special attention to what I'm about to say.

Nakir, Mukar: Yes, Master.

Lucifer: In fact, this will be your first lesson. Use her strongest virtue, honesty, to undermine her will to resist abortion. The thought of living a lie for the rest of her marriage, that's the thing, that's what will weaken her will. There's the genius of this tactic: Lead her to the point where her honesty works against her other virtues.

Nakir: But Master, if honesty is so important to her, why doesn't she simply tell her husband that she's been unfaithful to him and that she's not sure who the baby's father is?

Munkar: Yes, Master, why not? Then she'd be freed from her dilemma of deceit versus abortion.

Lucifer: Why not? Because, angels, one's strength is also one's weakness. My guess – and you may be sure it's a shrewd one – is that since childhood, Mrs. Crawford's been praised for her moral integrity. Her sense of being a woman of virtue is now inextricably part of her self-identity. The irony of this is that in her fixation on being virtuous, she has cultivated, with our help, I'm sure, the vice of pride. So she can't bear the thought of revealing her sinfulness to her husband, the thought of him seeing her and her seeing herself, as a sinner. And that's not the only threat to her pride. If her confession of infidelity causes him to divorce her, everyone else will see that she wasn't the virtuous woman they thought she was.

Munkar: Oh, Master, how brilliant!

Nakir: Yes, your tactics are magnificent. Master, how can Michael ever hope to get the better of you?

Lucifer: You know, angel, you have a point there. Well! Back to business. What I want you to take from this instruction is the importance of discerning both the strength and weakness of a soul and then using that strength to your advantage.

Nakir, Munkar: Yes, Master.

Lucifer: One more thing. I won't tolerate failure. If Mabel Crawford does not abort her child, rest assured your future assignments will be less than pleasant

Munkar: We won't fail you, Master.

Baalberith: Your meeting with Master Lucifer is over. Depart.

Nakir, Munkar: As you command, sir.

Lucifer: Wait until Michael gets news of our plans for Mrs. Crawford, eh Baalberith! I wonder what he'll do, that swaggering puppet...

****

Pablo: Commander, we came as soon as we heard that you called for Ling and me.

Ling: Metraton told us to report directly to you for an important mission.

Michael: I appreciate your prompt response. Metraton has enthusiastically recommended you both. I need you Ling because you've had unrivalled experience protecting women from the demons' efforts to persuade them to abort their unborn.

Ling: Yes, Commander, but with mixed success, I'm afraid.

Michael: True, but, thanks to the dedication and efforts of you and other angels, we're winning.

Ling: Yes, Sir, although progress has been slow, it's clear to us that the number of women we succeed in bringing to resist the temptation to abort their unborn continues to increase.

Michael: Good. I'd like you to protect Mabel Crawford who is about to suffer intense temptation to have an abortion. It seems that Lucifer has taken a special interest in her case. He's assigned Nakir and Mukar to it.

Pablo: Sir, I speak from experience when I say they're formidable adversaries. I've never faced them both together, but I have faced each individually on many occasions. They're adept at surmising what people think and feel just from watching their behavior and facial expressions and listening to what they say. Together, they'll be a formidable combination.

Michael: And *that*, Pablo, is precisely why you're needed for the mission. From all reports, nobody knows the *modus operandi* of those two demons better than you. If Nakir and Mukar will be doubly potent working as a team, I've every confidence that you and Ling together will prove to be equally potent.

Ling: Commander, rest assured we'll do our best.

Michael: I'm sure you will. But don't forget, we are all servants of God's providence. We have no way of knowing what, in his infinite love and wisdom, he has in store for Mabel Crawford. Do your best and trust always in him.

Ling, Pablo: Yes, Commander.

10

EYE OF THE STORM

Lucifer: Well, Michael, I'm sure you've noticed that Ling has bungled a stellar opportunity to persuade Mabel Crawford not to peruse the Yellow Pages for abortion clinics. He assumed she was interested in checking the entertainment section to find some event that would help take her mind off her crisis. So instead of discouraging her from consulting the book, he encouraged her inclination to open it. I always thought he was a naïf, too quick to see the good in people. Nakir, on the contrary, is more astute – I personally trained him. He correctly surmised that she was rationalizing, telling herself that there was nothing wrong with getting an idea of the abortion scene. Not that she had any intention of getting an abortion, understand; it was just idle curiosity. Step by step, we'll get Mrs. Virtue to the abortionist.

Michael: I can't deny it; Ling's misjudgment was unfortunate. But she's still a long way from getting an abortion. His mistake is a setback, but it can be rectified. Besides, Ling's a quick study; I'm confident that he's already learned from it. I notice you make no mention of the success Pablo is having in countering Mukar's efforts to intensify Crawford's fears of what her husband will do if she tells him she doesn't know who the father is. Another thing I notice is…

Lucifer: Michael, Michael. Look at us, vying with each other for Mabel Crawford's soul. All the plotting and maneuvering. What's happened to us? Remember when we were friends?

Michael: When *we* were friends? I remember when *I* was *your* friend.

****

Ingram Content Group UK Ltd.
Milton Keynes UK
UKHW011257230623
423944UK00001B/169

9 781425 136529